MIRROR

MIRROR

KENZIE DAWN

MIЯROR

Book one of the MIЯROR series.

Published by Kenzie Dawn
& Intelligible Ink

To those who think they're too much.
And not enough.

Which are, really, the same fears.

Man shouldn't be able to see his own face—there's nothing more sinister. Nature gave him the gift of not being able to see it, and of not being able to stare into his own eyes.

Only in the water of rivers and ponds could he look at his face. And the very posture he had to assume was symbolic. He had to bend over, stoop down, to commit the ignominy of beholding himself.

The inventor of the mirror
poisoned the human heart.

— FERNANDO PESSOA,
"The Book of Disquiet"

AUTHOR'S NOTE

After a long year of soul searching, writer's block, and trying to force my New Adult writing style into a Young Adult book, I finally remembered who I am, and what I write.

And what I'm best at.

Because of the younger audience, I was terrified to include the heavy details necessary to this story—even in the subplot. I forgot that darkness is a part of life.

And most importantly, I forgot the reason I wanted to write it at all:

It's a story I needed as a teen.

As a young adult.

On the surface, it's a conceptual, trippy novel that can be enjoyed by all ages.

But beneath is a story that showcases the terror of being human, of being powerless, and perhaps that's why it was so impossible to write until it had to be written.

MIЯROR began as a speculative thriller; a story that was as intriguing as it was creepy, but it lacked the sort of impact that would make readers sit in silence for a few moments after the end.

MIЯROR developed that impact as I watched the people around me and took a good, long look at my own insecurities and mindsets.

It became a love letter of sorts:

To my past self, who hated her reflection.

To the ones who lock away their pieces, afraid to be *too much* or *too little*. Who experience in two conflicting fears the exact same thing: the anxiety of being exposed.

And finally, to everyone who needs to be seen.

What better way to write about such things than in a story about a mirror?

While writing, MIЯROR touched on sensitive topics I didn't know existed, blindsided me with a self-awareness I never asked for (but I'm glad I've found).

It came to embody two of my favorite quotes:

"Art should comfort the disturbed
and disturb the comfortable."
— Caesar Cruz

"The thing you are most afraid to write:
Write that."
— Nayyirah Waheed

So I hope, when you read it, that you find a piece of yourself in the pages.

That it makes you laugh.

That it makes you uncomfortable.

That it makes you cry.

And if nothing else: that it's an unnervingly speculative read.

If you want stories with happy endings, I'm afraid you'll need to look elsewhere.

If you want slow descents into madness, unreliable narrators, and complicated, chaotic villains with more emotion than they know what to do with …

You're in the right place.

TABLE OF CONTENTS

ONE

In Which We Meet the Watcher

Look at her.

Worn sweatshirt, grey sweats. Her socks are stretched out and falling down around her ankles, and she uses one foot to itch her other calf, nearly toppling herself in the process.

The converted attic she stands in has been done up in pretty pinks and blues and greens.

Her friends—the three people she cares for most in this world—scurry around, readying for yet another summer slumber party.

Her own movements are slower:

Though she tries to hide it, she moves as though even the smallest action—a bend at the knees to reach the decoration she dropped, a turn of the head to smile at her friends, a stretch upward to hang the "karaoke" banner—sends a million slivers of pain through her.

It does.

You see: my world is not meant for human beings. That doesn't stop them from entering, of course, but it always, *always* stops their escape.

Except hers.

She was just a child—nine years old, when she broke her grandmother's mirror and its creatures emerged to pull her inside.

When she met me.

I was thrilled to have another playmate—most humans who find themselves in my world dissolve within hours, minds too frail to handle the way the mirror fractures and reflects and proliferates them.

Maia was a new thing, though: special.

I could tell just by looking at her.

I told her, *Let's play a game.*

Hide-and-seek, she called it, once I explained the rules.

I'll hide, I suggested, already beginning to disappear into the mirror's shadows. *And you seek.*

What actually happened had a simpler name:

Hide.

She never found me.

I don't believe she ever even cared to *look*.

Instead, she somehow found a way out, fracturing and destroying pieces of my perfect world in her wake, and I was left alone.

Again.

What a clever thing she is.

I was like her, once.

Long ago.

But it's not so bad here, you know?

I watch from the antique mirror that stands at the back of the attic as the space practically *glows* with her friends' mirth, and I ignore the bright flashes of envy that flare at the base of my rib cage when she laughs with them.

Soon enough, she will be back where she belongs. The mirror world will contain another living thing, and I will have someone to play with.

For at least as long as she lasts.

A shrieking laugh pulls my mind back to the scene at hand:

Lucy Thatcher, clad in an awful pink onesie that resembles a blob of cotton candy more than the dragon I fear it was meant to, is bouncing—full to the brim with more sugar than her 16-year-old body can handle. A tail bobs behind her as she sets out more treats.

Rylee Monroe scrolls through the settings on her phone, desperate to connect it to the speaker on the snack table before the other guests arrive.

June Marley, makeup already smudged at the corners of her eyes from laughing so hard she cried when she first saw Lucy's outfit, tells Rylee how to navigate the simple wireless connection.

And Maia Hartley.

Beautiful, charming, sweet Maia.

She flits between her friends like a hummingbird, never still for more than a moment, laughter like a contagion.

There's something not quite right about her—a darkness she hides. It makes her smiles seem timid and her laughter, contagious as it may be, seem forced.

Unless you know her like I do, though, you'd never know:

She's too good at hiding it.

June's makeup is running again. Rylee's frustration is at an all-time high. Lucy snaps a selfie with Maia.

And Maia never looks at me.

It's been so long since I've been on the outside, I can't recall if you can see past your own reflection to the thing—the *world*—that hides behind it.

Regardless, Maia avoids the mirror like she knows I'm watching, cautious to never stray too near.

It's quite rude that she pretends I don't exist.

The doorbell rings, and the girls race each other down the attic stairs and then the main ones.

Lucy nearly trips on her dragon tail.

June bursts into another fit of laughter.

They welcome their guests with open arms, and as the evening wears on, the attic cramps with more girls, all wearing various shades of eye-splitting color.

It's a tradition—these summertime Friday night parties. Maia suggested the idea near the end of ninth grade after Lucy made an offhand comment about summer being the loneliest time of the year:

"Think about it," she'd said, sipping on a bright blue slushie. "You get to see your friends almost every single day during the school year, and there are always parties and get-togethers over Christmas break … but there's nothing in the summer."

"Then I guess we'll have to do something—once a week." Maia linked arms with June as they walked through the 7-Eleven parking lot.

I watched from its streaked windows that day.

"Like what—a party?" June said sarcastically.

"Exactly."

"I was kidding."

"I'm not! We'll do different themes and whatever. You know, like on Pinterest."

"Yeah, and where's all this partying going to take place, huh?" June jabbed. "Mr. and Mrs. Hudson are way too old to go for it."

"I'm going to tell Earl you said that."

"My attic is almost finished," Rylee piped up. "It's big enough that we could even invite other kids from school." She gasped, face brightening. "*And* after every party, you guys can sleep over!"

And so, for the second summer in a row, the four of them have taken over Mrs. Monroe's attic every Friday night and filled it with sugar and music and fun.

Rylee finally manages to connect her phone to the speaker and the mirror's frame vibrates around me as music blares through the attic.

To my eternal shock, neither her mother nor her big brother, Teddy, come to lessen the noise, so I'm stuck in a shivering antique frame with nothing to do but watch as the girls pass a hairbrush around as if it were a microphone.

That's a lie.

I have much to do: arrangements to make, creatures to stage, another game to set …

But curiosity overwhelms me, and I can do nothing but sit behind this mirror and watch, afraid to miss even a moment of this night:

It marks the end of Maia's allotted seven years.

That's the funny thing about your mirror saying.

You know—the one that says when you break a mirror, you'll have seven years of bad luck.

I suppose the reason no one ever tells you *why* is because no one has ever come back to.

Not whole, anyway:

Maia may be the only one who has ever escaped, but sometimes, for a bit of fun, the mirror will allow me to let one out.

They're the ones that fill your asylums. The ones that stand on street corners, holding signs with funny phrases like, "The end of times is near!"

They're the ones so twisted and broken and crimped they don't recognize their own reflections.

The mirror's pull is an inescapable, irresistible thing—and it always takes them back after seven years.

How Maia has been able to withstand it for so long astounds me.

No one fights the mirror and wins.

She piqued my intrigue beyond obsession when she escaped, and I watched her entire life like a TV show—went all the way back to Season One to bring myself up to speed:

I was in the patch of black ice when her parents died in a horrific accident on a snowy road. She was only seven when she watched their caskets lowered into the icy ground.

She then lived with her grandmother, and accidentally broke a mirror when she was nine. Not even a full year after her escape, I watched from the clock face on the hospital wall as her grandmother passed away.

She was thrust into the whirlwind of the foster care system; tossed around like a leaf on the breeze.

The breeze died when she moved in with the Hudsons—an elderly couple without children of their own—and I watched from the polished courthouse floor when they adopted her only eleven months after meeting her.

And then came her friends:

She met June first, and after the feisty 11-year-old Marley girl broke Tommy Williams's nose for telling Maia she looked like she came from a donation pile, the girls became fast friends.

Rylee's friendship came next when she helped Maia understand the difference between *omniscient* and *limited* points of view in the seventh-grade English class Maia was close to failing.

Lucy moved into the empty house near Rylee's in ninth grade, and Maia, June, and Rylee—already thick as thieves—befriended her by delivering a plate of cookies.

Lucy befriended *them* by pretending the cookies were any good.

I may not be a mind reader, but I can watch any moment of any life from any reflective surface: the glass of picture frames, a droplet of water falling from a roof corner, the facets of your jewelry.

The view is distorted through things like tile floors and polished countertops and metal fixtures and oven doors, but when it comes right down to it, I can watch through those as well.

I can see any moment, past or present.

I can rewind, slow down, speed up, pause.

I can watch from any angle.

Multiple angles.

All angles simultaneously, if it suits me.

So I may not be a mind reader …

But I can watch until I know you better than you know yourself.

And yet, after all this time,

I still don't know how Maia escaped.

I sigh, long and dramatic—to myself (and you) for effect—and it echoes in the world behind me, bouncing off the mirror's wandering creatures.

I am not always this … how would you say it …

Moody.

In fact, I'm usually quite fun.

I press my face and hands to the backside of Mrs. Monroe's antique mirror like a child, stand on tiptoe to see over the party guests' heads.

Maia is at the edge, as far away from me and the mirror as she can get.

Displeased is an understatement.

Lucy's face brightens. Over the blaring music, she yells, "Rylee, Rylee! Do June's song!"

June giggles in mock horror. "Please don't."

"Please *do!*" Maia drags June to the makeshift stage in the middle of the room: a small circle hemmed by mismatched pillows.

Rylee scrolls through the playlist as Lucy starts the girls chanting: "June's song! June's song! June's song!"

Madonna's *Material Girl* bursts through the speaker.

I should mention that the speaker in question is pointed directly at *me*, and though a pane of silvered glass separates me from Maia's world, the noise is deafening.

June continues her protests—she's the friend everyone seems to have who scorns attention just to get more.

As soon as the first verse begins, she becomes the performer her mother raised her to be.

I would know, because I was in the black reflection of their TV screen when her mother taught her lyrics and choreography. They would dance circles around the living room together, long before her mother's cancer spread.

June leaps onto the attic's threadbare couch for the second verse, displacing the girls sitting on it.

Maia laughs, and I feel a slight warmth.

She took a piece of the mirror with her when she escaped, and it connects the two of us across the boundary between worlds.

It's a little prickling thing, as fragile as a string of blown glass, as small as a crack in a door left ajar.

It doesn't allow me access to her thoughts, nor to her every emotion, but every once in a while, she feels things so strongly they reach all the way across the boundary between worlds to me.

I felt her grief when her grandmother died. Her hope when she met the Hudsons. Her joy among her friends.

The girls collapse into a fit of laughter. Lucy hollers, "Who wants more snacks?!"

A familiar pull tugs at the edges of my awareness.

I turn my full attention back to the party to find Maia—still at the far edge of the attic—staring directly at me.

I grin.

Something pulls at the space between us, tightening it like a spoke.

She looks at her own reflection as though she can't help it, gaze anchored despite the flurry of motion between us.

My grin stretches into a smile.

She can't see me—can't feel the thing that connects us.

I know, because when June bumps into her side on the way to the snack table, Maia turns from me as though nothing happened.

She smiles at June. Laughs with Rylee. She picks the red gummy bears out of the bowl on the snack table and splits them with Lucy.

To anyone who knows her less than I do, she looks like an ordinary teenage girl: average height, typical grades, familiar group of friends.

Aside from the faint rings of violet that surround her pupils—aftereffects of her visit to the mirror world—there is nothing special about her on the outside.

But the mirror's power—*my* power, to create and unwind and reshape—has grown in her veins for all the years since her escape.

It's the reason she moves like a person hiding their pain. I can feel it when she bolts upright at night.

It screams down the connection between us like a runaway train—an insistent tug on each organ, a scraping on the inside of each bone, a mounting pressure in the skull.

More nights than not, she locks herself in the bathroom, retching because it's the only way she can think to purge the intrusion.

It's futile.

There's no outlet for such power in her world, and without the mirror, it will grow with no release.

The poor girl doesn't even know what it is that shifts beneath her skin.

And when the mirror finally pulls her back inside, when the pressure it applies to fracture and reflect and proliferate its prey begins to crack her open—

I might have a worthwhile game to play at last.

TWO

The Threshold of Seven Years

I watch from the living room windows as June closes the front door behind the last party guest and trudges back up the stairs, exhaustion tugging at her feet. She flops into the mountain of pillows Rylee pushed against a wall and throws an arm over her eyes. “Okay, you were right. Karaoke is still cool, I guess.”

Lucy takes advantage of June’s blindness and slams a pillow over her head. “I *told* you.”

June slaps it away to reveal a scowl that could kill the dead.

Rylee stuffs trash into a garbage bag. “Girls, girls, you’re both pretty,” she murmurs.

June and Lucy share a brief, mischievous glance before pelting her with pillows from both sides. She yelps and swings the garbage bag at Lucy's knees.

Lucy trips on her dragon tail in her attempt to escape—the physics of it astounds me; the thing is quite literally *behind* her—and flails headlong into the cushion pile.

Rylee and June team up in the tussle, walloping her with pillows as she giggles and tries to fend them off.

She unzips a pillow and throws a handful of feathers, using the diversion to scramble away on her hands and knees.

June grabs her tail— "Oh no you don't!"

Lucy turns and stuffs another handful in June's face. She makes a narrow escape.

And her forward momentum carries her directly towards *me*.

Maia appears at the top of the attic stairs.

Her face pales when she sees Lucy's trajectory.

I hold my breath.

Time seems to slow.

The spray bottle and rag fall from Maia's hands. They tumble down the stairs behind her.

She opens her mouth in warning at the same time Lucy makes a hard left.

Lucy's shoulder grazes the edge of the mirror's frame.

It rocks.

Just a bit.

"*Lucy!*" Maia scolds, eyes wide with terror.

Her friends' boisterous laughter swallows the sound of her voice.

Lucy whaps June in the side. Rylee knocks Lucy over the head with the open pillow in an explosion of feathers.

Maia waves a hand through the mess, clearing the air with only enough time to wedge herself between her friends and me as the fight trespasses too close to the mirror's fragile glass.

"*Hey, stop that!*" Maia yells. "You'll *break* it!"

I giggle a little, surprising myself:

It's the closest she's come to a mirror in seven full years.

Maia's fear ratchets up and up and up until I can taste it—like the bitter tang of rotten berries.

It morphs and spreads and mutates and fogs until even I choke.

"*Stop it!*" Maia commands again, but the girls are so lost in their own giggles, they don't hear her.

Lucy's swing at Rylee goes wide, putting Maia and I directly in the pillow's path.

Maia ducks it just in time.

I, too, duck. Because even though there's a pane of glass between me and the girls, a pillow enroute directly to the face is still a bit alarming.

The corner thumps against the mirror's frame as Lucy's swing completes its circle.

The frame wobbles.

My pulse jumps.

I can almost *feel* the shattering that will bring Maia back to me.

The sound of it echoes in my ears.

The anticipation is a shiver down my arms, up my spine.

I find myself bouncing on the balls of my feet.

But Maia, clever little thing that she is, notices the sway too soon.

She halts it before storming over to the speaker on the table.

My anger is palpable.

I can taste it on my tongue. Feel it in the vibrations of my fingers as they curl into fists.

I take a noisy breath and count to ten—something Maia does when she's scared—and continue watching.

After all, her return is imminent. It's merely the wait that has my blood boiling.

She turns off the music. "*Listen to me,*" she snarls.

Her friends pause mid-fight, blinking at her.

Her hostility is a side she never allows to see the light, and its appearance on a night like tonight is breathtaking in its danger.

The silence is blaring.

"Don't. Break. Mirrors," Maia articulates, a curiously venomous mix of fear and longing in each word as she stalks toward her friends.

"*Everyone* says that! They never tell you why—"

Lucy tries to bump Maia's hip with her pillow.

Maia rips it away. "*Give me that!*"

The girls hold their breath.

Maia's heartbeat is visible at the base of her throat.

She sighs. Tension bleeds out of her body a piece at a time.

She returns Lucy's pillow and forces a strained laugh—as though such a simple thing might reconcile the moment.

And then she says the one thing I never expected to hear tonight: "I gotta go."

My chest seizes.

There isn't a mirror in her room. There are no mirrors in her entire house other than in the master bathroom—the result of a panic attack in junior high, during which her fear of them became starkly evident.

If she leaves now … No. I won't allow it. The *mirror* won't allow it.

Through the thing that connects us, I feel her fight its pull. She hides the tremor in her hands by grabbing her backpack and swinging it onto her shoulder. Pointing at her friends.

"More karaoke," she says. "Less pillow fighting."

She pauses a moment in the attic doorway and looks back like she might change her mind. A shadow passes behind her gaze. "I'll see you later."

And then. She leaves.

And I'm … stumped.

Angry.

I could have sworn tonight was the night.

I snap my fingers and a creature brings me a calendar. It takes only a moment to find what I'm looking for: Yes.

Tonight is the eve of Maia's eighth year.

At the turn of midnight, the boundary between my world and hers will close permanently.

The mirror gets what it wants.

It always has; it always will.

So why, then, am I standing behind a still-unbroken mirror in a room now Maia-less?

I fracture into two pieces:

One follows Maia as she leaves:

Her exit is nonchalant until she's out of her
friends' line of sight, then I watch through the
living room window as she nearly trips over her
own feet in her rush down the main stairs.

The other watches her friends as they stay:

Lucy is the first to break the tense silence in the wake of Maia's exit, her voice thick and swirling like she's underwater; the result of my attention divided.

"So … what's Maia's deal?"

"She has nightmares." Rylee's voice wavers with worry as she looks at the open attic door. "I think it embarrasses her, so she never stays to sleep over after the parties— I thought you knew that?"

Maia stomps down the porch stairs,
down the driveway,
down the street,
like every step matters.

Like if she can just put
a step
a step
a step
a step
between herself
and the mirror, it will get easier
each time she lifts her foot.

"Of course I know that," Lucy responds, rolling her eyes, "she told me in Chem lab once. I meant, what's her deal with the mirror?" She knocks a knuckle against the glass, jarringly fusing my split attention, snapping it back to the attic.

I scowl at her round face—level with mine.

She has yet to outgrow her baby pudge.

"Oh, that," Rylee says.

"I mean … it's pretty and all, but it's not even hers—" Lucy catches the expression on Rylee's face. "What, is she scared of them or something?" she jokes.

June wriggles her fingers in Rylee's face. "Don't break a mirror or you'll get seven years of *bad luck*." She pops a piece of rogue popcorn in her mouth as Rylee bats her away.

"Stop it, June."

"Obviously, June." Lucy rolls her eyes.

Rylee picks up the trash bag again. "What's your biggest fear, Luce?" she asks.

"Oh, snakes: easy."

"Like our own little Indiana Jones," June teases.

Lucy frowns, likely remembering her horror at the scene from the trilogy they marathoned last summer. "Oh yeah?" she counters. "What's yours, then?"

I smile, because I know.

I fracture again, unwilling to miss even a moment:

There's an uncontrollable darkness that leaks
from Maia's side of our connection as the
mirror's pull increases.
It consumes all her rational thought.

It screams two separate desires:

On the one hand:
to get away,
to go *home.*

On the other:
to go back,
to go *in.*

She feels them so strongly, so uncontrollably, that they force the doorway between us wider. Just wide enough that if I try, I can even catch small snippets of her thoughts, insubstantial and yet heavy to retrieve. They fritz and pop like a bad radio signal:

I can

not.

This is

not …

right left right left
Keep walking, Maia.

She stops mid-stride.

I can't go home.

The thought is louder than the others: the
first crystal-clear thing I've ever heard from
her. Her shoulders bend beneath the weight of
it. Her mind projects an image of the mirror in
the Hudsons' master bathroom, and I can feel
the way she *knows* she won't be able to stop
herself from shattering any mirror
in her proximity.

After all,
it doesn't have to be an antique.

It doesn't need to have
a specific frame
in a specific place
at a specific time.

Any mirror will do.

Maia plants her feet,
her will ironclad, and thinks:

I can't go home.

June shrugs at Lucy's question, and as nonchalantly as someone can admit such a heavy fear, she states: "Being forgotten."

Rylee pauses her cleaning. "Yikes …" she says, taking her time on the *Y*. "Way to take a downturn for the night."

June shrugs again. "We're not little girls anymore, Rylee. Fears grow as we do."

Lucy smacks June in the back with a pillow. "Who knew June Marley was such a poet?"

"Yeah, yeah. I'll wring your neck if you tell anyone. I've got a reputation to uphold, you know."

Lucy frowns and drops her arms to her sides, the pillow dangles between them. "What's Maia's?"

"Music boxes," June says.

"Oooookaaaaaaay …" Lucy prompts. "Is there more to *that* story?"

"If there is, I don't know it."

The mirror's gravity
is a steady pull against
Maia's persistence.

She buckles down even tighter—
locks every muscle in place.

She won't go back to the attic.

She will not go home.

Until midnight, she will not go anywhere.

If I look hard enough through the
windows of houses that line the street,
I can see flutters of pulsing veins in her wrists,
tiny tremors in her legs, like they'll walk her
back to Rylee's themselves.

My excitement for Maia to reenter the mirror is
so at odds with her rising terror that the duality of it
makes me feel three things I haven't felt in years:

Pity.

A sense of melancholy that no matter how hard
she fights, she'll end up right back where she started.

And a tiny sliver of mercy …

If I were the mirror, perhaps I would leave her
alone: a reward for her refusal to yield.

Rylee checks her reflection in the attic mirror. She's the smallest of the group, so at least I'm not staring her in the face. She yawns and threads her fingers through her hair, frowning when they tangle. "Can we go to bed yet?"

"Aw, c'mon, seriously?" Lucy wails. "It's *summer*, Ry. And only eleven"—she taps Rylee's phone screen on the snack table—"thirty-two. When did you get so *lame?*"

"Rylee's always been lame," June smirks. "You can either be smart or you can be cool."

Rylee purses her lips as if to say, *You're not funny.*

June pokes her in the shoulder. "Don't think we'll let you off the hook so easily, Rylee Monroe." She smirks. "What's *your* biggest fear?"

Rylee prods at the imaginary circles under her eyes. "The lack of sleep I'm getting."

"Very funny."

"Fine, fine." She hesitates. Shifts on her feet.

"Dolls—"

"Still?"

"*June.*"

"I guess not everyone's fears grow with them."

Rylee frowns. She motions to the pillows strewn across the floor. "Bed? *Please?*"

"Yeah"—June's smirk turns devilish—"sure, *Grandma.* Let's go to bed."

She snatches a pillow from the floor and swings it into Rylee's stomach.

Hard.

I see the inevitability only moments before it happens, and I'm so entranced by it that my focus slips away from Maia.

The mirror's creatures even pause their wandering to watch:

Rylee loses her balance.

Her back touches the mirror's glass.

It's just a feather's weight at first—a brush of her pajama top against the smooth surface …

And then the glass cracks at the point of impact, spiderwebbing to the corners.

June grabs Rylee by the elbow to keep her from falling to the floor, but the damage has been done.

My vision shatters.

Drops out of the antique frame.

Sprays across the attic floor.

And instead of looking at Maia's friends through a standing, single mirror, I look up at them through its pieces.

They are, unsurprisingly, much taller from this angle.

I laugh in delight; this turn of events so unexpected.

The mirror turns its attention toward the girls.

"*June*," Rylee stammers, "my parents are going to *kill* me! That mirror is an antique! And probably worth, like … more money than you'll ever see in your entire *life!*"

Mrs. Monroe's voice floats up from the floor below. "Rylee?" she calls groggily, half-asleep. "What's going on up there?"

I could see her, if I wish—see if she's cognizant enough to venture upstairs and ruin my fun. There are a total of four mirrors in her room and the adjoining bathroom.

Why don't I?

Because Maia's left foot
turns back toward Rylee's.

Her body shudders once,
like a glitch.

Her right foot follows her left,
sneaker scraping against the asphalt
as she tries to drag it back.

Rylee hits the attic light switch, eyes wide at her mother's voice.

"Shoot, shoot, shoot, shoot, *shoot!*" She closes the attic door. "Bedtime—both of you. For *real* this time. And *be quiet.*"

Lucy takes the couch. Rylee and June gather a mishmash of pillows on the floor and throw a blanket over themselves.

The room falls silent.

And outside on the street,
Maia begins her excruciating journey
back to the mirror.

THREE

Here You Will Be Safe

The girls are quick to fall asleep.

The tune of the music box begins so quietly that even in the realm of wakefulness you wouldn't hear it. It crescendos until it seeps through the cracks in the girls' dreams, reaches inside and tugs them awake.

It's the mirror's gentle greeting: a thing that says *Welcome,* and *You are not alone.*

It's what the mirror does, you see:

It watches you look into it with such negativity—such doubt and loathing for your own reflection.

It lures you with everything opposite.

The antique frame stands empty, unassuming. Harmless.

Until it isn't.

The air inside shivers once.

Twice.

Quicker.

And I will never get tired of this part:

The air quivers once more, and from the flutter crawls a creature.

A thing of shadow, of memory, of thought. A thing that moves with glitching human form, as though the creator's program can't yet sustain it fully.

Another steps out behind it.

A third follows, and then another, until their movements are fluid, the skin of their bodies like the reflective surface of oil in the moonlight through the attic windows.

They surround the sleeping girls … and wait.

Maia walks back to Rylee's
like a prisoner to the gallows.
I abandon her to her slow journey,
confident that there's nothing
she can do to escape her fate now.

Besides …
I have new toys that need my attention.

A deep, human instinct of being watched prods Lucy awake first.

She sits up in a daze and shakes her head, gaze drawn to the mirror at the back of the attic.

She gets to her feet and tiptoes across the wooden attic floor on bare feet, toes only inches from the sharp glass as she stands before the mirror.

She looks at her reflection, and it doesn't occur to her that there shouldn't be one.

The creature in the mirror extends a hand, fingers uncurling like vines.

Lucy blinks slowly.

She places her hand in its own, and the creature pulls—just a tug.

A suggestion.

She disappears into the mirror without a trace.

More creatures pour through the frame's opening, spilling over each other. The shimmering air casts iridescence around the room like light refracted from water's surface.

They surround Rylee next, draw her up from the floor. She sways on her feet, still halfway clutched by sleep's grasp. A creature brushes a hand past her face, and she wakes like a thing come to life.

The creatures smile, mouths pulling wide.

Come, they urge. *Follow*, they press.

Their voices weave through the hiss of the late summer storm that brews outside, the whistle of wind and crackle of electricity.

Rylee doesn't think to look at June still asleep on the floor.

It doesn't strike her as odd that Lucy is gone.

She returns the creatures' grins dreamily, and the mirror reaches out to take her, leaving nothing behind but a ripple to show that someone was once there.

At once, the creatures' attention draws to June.

Her chest rises and falls slowly, evenly, unaware of what waits for her on the other side of waking.

One raises a dark, reflective arm, and her body shudders, as though even in sleep, unaware of the risk surrounding her, she fights their allure.

Another creature joins, and June lifts from the ground as though held by invisible arms.

Her head cants back, throat exposed, like they forgot to support her neck.

It isn't until a third creature joins—the mirror's pull unbearable, its pressure electric in the enclosed space—that June rotates upright.

Her body straightens from its bent angles until she balances on the tips of her toes like a puppet held just a hair too far above the ground.

The creatures slink around her—the mirror's way of playing with its prey.

One gets right in her face, nose to nose.

She jolts awake.

Her body remembers the reality of gravity with a crash, buckling her knees.

She's quick—a fighter.

And before she even crumples fully to the floor, she's rolling away from the outstretched arms that reach for her.

She whips her head from side to side, gaze racing over the scattered pillows and empty blankets.

Her chest heaves, and on instinct, she bolts.

She isn't awake enough yet to calculate the space she has for such a maneuver and slams into a creature.

The room bursts with them; the things are on the walls, in the corners, near the ceiling, in the window.

Everywhere she turns, they wait.

A creature closes a hand around her arm. She jerks out of its grasp and backs into another. I feel her terror through the mirror's grasp as it ratchets to a shrill peak.

She goes into overdrive—cuts a path through the creatures as they yank her hair and snatch at her clothing and pinch and press and squeeze and grab.

In the end, though, she too goes through the mirror:

The serene darkness beyond, empty of creatures, beckons in a way that says: *Here you will be safe.*

And she dives through like it's her last hope.

FOUR

Welcome

I uncoil like a spider in preparation for the girls' arrival—reach my long fingers to the very edges of the mirror world, weave them through its fabric until I can pull one tiny string and create something entirely new.

The sensation is like a good stretch after a long nap. I wait with bated breath for the last of my new playmates.

It doesn't take long.

June breaks through the rift at full tilt.

Her desperate momentum crashes her into Rylee and Lucy, both of whom are gaping.

The three of them go down in a tangled heap.

June scrambles to her feet. She pulls Lucy up by the elbow, helps Rylee up by the shoulders.

Eyes wide and desperate, she pats at their faces. "Lucy?" she pants. "Rylee, are you alright? What are you doing here?"

Lucy's mouth bobs like a fish as she blinks at the world around them, so abruptly different from the attic.

Rylee rubs her arms, voice trembling. "Where *is* … here?"

The startling thud of stage lights starts at their backs and thump thump thumps past them.

Beams of bright purple and blue streak through a swirling sheen of haze.

There is no discernable floor.

No ceiling.

No walls.

The vision of Maia's friends—here, of all places—is still so unexpected I have the absurd urge to laugh.

Lucy's pink dragon onesie fits right in among the mirror's chaos and color.

Rylee's long golden hair catches the sweeping light.

The beams cut lazily through the haze in a pattern that suggests an overture.

I suppose you could say I have a flair for showmanship.

June turns in a slow circle, mouth agape.

Lucy taps her toe against the non-ground to find a stark resistance—like a floor. She frowns, because there is nothing of the sort.

"Tell me you guys are seeing this." Her voice echoes in the vast space. "Or"—she reconsiders—"*not* seeing it."

June crouches to touch it and her hand passes through. Her fingers wiggle beneath her toes. She pulls her hand back, shakes it a little.

"How is this even *possible?*"

The mirror secretly tugs at the girls' jitters, yanks their unease into the open. It fissures their minds just enough to find the things they fear the most.

It feeds me their fears, and in the shadows, I create them.

My fingers flutter at my sides as I twist the mirror's creatures, readying for what will be the most entertaining game I've ever played.

The clinking reaches Rylee's ears before the sight does.

"Do you hear that?" She tips her head to the side.

June and Lucy pause.

"Yeah," Lucy whispers.

June stands, wipes her hands on her thighs. "Hear what?"

Rylee squints at the shadows that stir at the edge of the light.

"Seriously, I don't hear anything," June says.

Rylee stumbles back a step as *things* come out of the darkness, the tick of their joints like teacups clinking, the chink of their footsteps an alarming cacophony in the silence.

Lucy makes a noise at the back of her throat as she sees them, too. She watches their bodies slide along the non-floor in a tangled weave of slinking scales, an accompanying hiss like the slide of a ballgown over tile. Her body shudders into an unwilling stillness, trapped in her own skin, unable to move away from them as they get closer.

And closer.

And closer.

June sees nothing but shadows; the outlines of humanoid figures so vague they're a mere suggestion of presence in the mirror's neon.

Lucy smacks June's arm and turns her around, pointing at the creatures that have fenced them in from behind.

"June?" Rylee's squeak is nearly lost beneath the clatter of joints as dolls of porcelain and wood and china approach. She grips June's wrist.

I separate them between one blink and the next—isolate them with their own fears until they can't see each other through the mob.

Rylee opens and closes her hand around the empty air where June's wrist was.

"*June!*" she screams. She whips her head around and is met with only painted faces. "Lucy!"

The creatures' whispers drown her out.

They're saying *Welcome.*

They're saying *We're glad to have you.*

They're saying *What scares you?*

We love you.

We hate you.

We'll make you—

Serpents wrap around Lucy's ankles. Her knees. Her hips. Waist. Shoulders.

She gasp—

gasp—

gasps—

at the size of them.

At the plump weight sliding over her shoulders.

June stands on her toes, desperate to push the shadows away, to find her friends in the expanse. She makes little progress against the endless sea, and finally settles flatfoot—much better for fighting.

She stops pulling punches.

"Lucy!" she yells. "Rylee!"

The creatures tug and pull at Rylee, tiny nips and tucks until she's perfect, the effect not unlike pulling a delicate splinter or needle out of skin, the flesh puckering before the edges are snipped away.

Fingers prod at her eyelids, stretch them until her eyes are oversized in her petite face. The hollows around her eyes deepen, lips thin into a baby-doll pout.

Her skin pales until it's plaster white, the only color left a bloom of blush high on her cheeks.

Scaled creatures slither over and against Lucy's skin. They squeeze until she can't breathe, until the space between their bodies and hers bleeds together; their scales become her own.

And June still fights.

At least until she, too, notices a change.

She yelps and jerks her left arm away from the creature she'd swung at. From the elbow down, her hand dissipates until her fingers are nothing but a suggestion of mass, invisible except for the faint outline that catches the neon light.

She blinks at it like she can't remember what her hand is supposed to look like—that she's supposed to have one at all.

Her face slackens. She grabs her left hand with her right and shakes it wildly. "*Rylee!*" she screams. "*Lucy!*"

The flurry of creatures is incalculable, stretching far into the horizons.

Rylee's movements slow in lurches.

Lucy coils against the mirror's non-floor.

June's body is spotted with transparency and shadow, limbs all but vanished.

She blinks down at herself, a crease between her brows, as though trying to remember something.

The girls are three pinpoints of eerie stillness in the frenzied swarm.

A creature coaxes Rylee's perfect enamel mouth upward. *Smile*, the thing says, its voice the sound of a thousand others.

She is watching.

Rylee's plaster cracks as she frowns. Her mouth opens to form the *W* in "*Who?*"

The creature seals the crevices with a gentle touch, the thing itself turning to porcelain. Its eyes glance behind her, to where I watch from the shadows.

She, it whispers.

FIVE

Hold On

I check back in on Maia the moment her fingers wrap around the handle of Rylee's front door.

Her feet carry her past the mirror in the entryway, and a sharp, sudden sting pulses through the gateway between us as she realizes the tether is not taking her to just any mirror.

It pulls to the one in the attic.

She yanks against it.

She screams her fear and frustration so loudly I have no choice but to hear it now.

There are so many other mirrors in Rylee's house:

one in the entryway,

one in each of the three bathrooms,

one in Teddy's bedroom,

four in Mrs. Monroe's …

But the mirror pulls Maia to only one: the attic. Where her friends are.

Or rather, where they *were.*

I laugh at the dramatic irony.

She reaches the second-floor hallway and throws herself to the side, grasping the bathroom doorknob like she'll bust in and smash the mirror inside to spare her friends. She grips it so tightly I almost expect it to cave.

Her hold slips away.

She reaches the base of the attic stairs.

Her mind races through countless possibilities as she climbs, bombarding me with ways to explain to her friends why they must leave *now.*

To explain why she's even back in the first place.

She stands before the closed attic door like a wraith, deciding on a path of action—*any* path that will remove them from the mirror's reach when she goes through.

She pushes open the creaking door when she can't fight the pull anymore.

A flicker of confusion crosses her face at the darkness—her friends have never gone to bed so early.

"Hey, guys," she whispers, fingers fluttering against her sides.

She hides her internal struggle so well that if I didn't have access to the backside of it, I might not notice it at all. "Have you seen my phone?"

She is not a clever liar.

She squints at the shapes on the floor.

"Sorry in advance, but I'm turning the lights on."

She hits the switch, and they flicker to life.

I feel the shock roll through her at the things she expects but doesn't see:

Rylee's blinking eyes,

June's scowl,

Lucy still fast asleep.

And her terror at the thing she does:

The antique frame stands empty, as unobtrusive as a television that's been turned off. Broken glass scatters the floor beneath.

I do believe she's having trouble breathing.

"No."

The word is a hammer strike on an anvil. Like if she says it with enough finality, her friends will appear, safe and unharmed and still as ignorant of the mirror as they were when she left. "No, no, no—"

It becomes a chant as she drops to her knees.

"No, no, no—"

She digs through the scattered pillows and blankets on the floor like she thinks she'll smack into Lucy's arm. June's leg. She might accidentally pull Rylee's long hair as she rips blankets to the side.

"No, no, no—"

The hope that Rylee will walk up from her mom's room downstairs, or that June or Lucy might appear behind the open closet door is stifling. It clogs the connection between us. Steals all the breath from Maia's chest as she digs and digs and *digs.*

Her hand brushes against the bottom of the mirror's golden frame and she jerks away like she's been scalded.

Her fight drains.

It leaches from her muscles one by one until she sits back on her heels and hitches a couple of breaths.

"What have you done?" she whispers, as if her friends might hear.

The attic's silence is the only answer.

For a bizarre moment, I feel her wish Teddy would appear in the attic doorway. Or Mrs. Monroe.

Someone.

Anyone to fill the awful silence.

Despair bends her shoulders forward.

I glance at the glowing numbers on the speaker at the same moment she does:

11:58

She reinforces herself with anger:

At herself, for thinking it was better to leave her friends—get herself away from them if she couldn't fight the mirror's pull so it wouldn't take them, too.

At the mirror, for being so greedy.

And a small sliver for her friends, who should have just *listened.*

She stands and raises her right foot to step through the mirror's frame—

Her foot hovers.

The last digit on the speaker changes from 8 to 9, and she *pauses.*

Something in her instinctively jerks against the mirror's pull for a final time, as though she's so used to fighting, there is no other choice.

"Come on, Maia," she murmurs to herself against the tidal wave of fear crashing through her. "Take the step."

Twin tremors race through her blood:

The mirror pulls her *toward.*

Her human instinct to survive—to escape—to win—pulls her *away*.

"They're counting on you."

She drags in a breath and locks herself down like an iron prison—even the connection between us dims.

The last echo that slips through is one that says she remembers the mirror's cracking pressure:

She knows she'll be the only one that stands between it and her friends.

And she knows that once she steps in, she won't be coming back out.

"Hold on," she whispers. "I'm coming to get you."

Her right foot falls.

Her left foot follows.

The mirror world frac

tures.

SIX

The Tearoom

The mirror recognizes Maia the moment she breaks through its threshold. Like a crack of lightning, it goes after her, sensing she's the one who jilted it.

I've never felt it put this kind of pressure on a person so quickly.

But, as always, it does so surreptitiously.

Maia hardly blinks at the intrusion. The mirror creates fissures in her mind, searching for her worst fears. Her insecurities. Her doubts.

The still-swinging stage lights shift and flicker as she weaves through swirling mist. She flicks her gaze around, searches for any signs of her friends—jittery, flighty—like prey in the domain of its predator.

I was content to let her wander a while, but excitement gets the better of me.

I look at the nearest creature to check my reflection—there's always a bit of nervous anticipation when welcoming new guests.

There's even more, apparently, when welcoming old ones.

The creature transforms, its image mirroring me down to the last detail.

I smile at my reflection.

Of all the people I've watched throughout the years, the businesswomen are my favorite: sleek, elegant, fierce.

Perfect.

I smooth my hands over the crisp lines of my black suit—complete with all three pieces—and the creature mimics me.

It's like looking into an actual mirror.

I lean in and touch up my blood-red lipstick, smooth my blonde hair back into a high ponytail.

I even pull a clipboard and pen from the folded shadows of the mirror—slide some glasses onto my nose, for the full effect.

Then I step out from those same shadows,

and we come face to face, Maia and I.

She's so grown up now—as tall as I am.

For the first time since meeting her seven years

ago, I can stare her straight in the eyes.

And though I'd love to live in this moment, revel in the rush of the win, she's frowning at me.

Perhaps *frown* is a meager term for her expression.

Her glare is sharp as cut glass.

"*You.*" She packs so much hatred and derision into the word, it's instinctive to step away. Instead, I push my glasses up by the bridge and smile sweetly. Like any good businesswoman, there's a hint of artifice behind my grin. "I'm sorry, have we met?"

She blinks. Her mouth drops open. "Have … we *met?*" The confusion that clouds her eyes turns red-hot. "Are you *kidding?* You've been the source of my nightmares for *years*—"

"Ah, yes, hello," I interrupt.

The click of my pen is satisfying in her shocked silence. And do I detect a touch of abandonment in her expression? There would be a hint of it in my own if I were in her position—forgotten by something like me.

I turn my gaze down to the clipboard nestled in the crook of my arm and write a quick, meaningless note.

I can almost hear her bewilderment.

I glance up at her. Smile.

She stiffens as I push my index finger into her sternum. I dig my nail in, walk her backward.

My stilettos click on the checkered tile floor that unfolds beneath me as my fingers twitch at my side, and a chair slams Maia in the back of the knees so rapidly she buckles into it.

"Take a seat, kid."

I snap my fingers in her face. "*Yes*, I know you: you are an old pal of mine."

Her face screws up in disgust, and I haven't laughed so hard in ages.

I tell her this, and she looks at me like I'm insane—understandable, sure.

I poke her hard in the shoulder. "Come on, Hartley, you can't possibly tell me you didn't enjoy your last stay here. We had such *fun*."

A current runs from my finger into her skin and she jerks, the legs of her chair scrape back.

She watches with wide eyes as a table slides between us, draped with a heavy carmine cloth. A chandelier pieces together above.

The facets of cut crystals catch the mirror's neon light and refract it, casting pinpricks of color around the room like a disco ball.

Walls extend upward around us, their golden wallpaper satin and glossy. Candelabras line the perimeter. Pale candles flicker to life. Crystalline teacups and a glass kettle of amber tea shimmer into existence on the table.

I pull a second chair from the mirror's pleats, flip it around.

I take a seat across from her and lean my forearms on the back of the chair. Rest my cheek against my fist.

And smile.

Maia studies me and the arrangements with uncertainty. She doesn't look the least bit entranced.

A long moment passes before she speaks.

"What is this?" Her voice is strangely flat.

Bored, even.

The edge of my smile twitches as I gesture at the table. "Don't you know what a tea party looks like? Isn't this what old friends do to catch up?"

The crystal cups fill with tea at my behest.

"We're going to finish our game, Maia Hartley. But for now, you're going to sit quietly and play nice."

She spreads her hands on the tablecloth and begins to stand. "I don't have time for tea parties."

"Shhh." I put my finger to my lips.

Halfway to standing, Maia's body freezes. Her own finger snaps to her mouth, mirroring mine.

Her eyes frost with fear when she can't pull it away.

I point to the chair behind her and she lowers slowly back into place. A muscle flutters in her temple as she tries to fight my hold.

"You're going to sit quietly." I grin. "And play nice."

I release my hold only after she relaxes.

She works her jaw like she's trying to solve a problem. Finally, she says, "What is this place?"

I raise a brow.

"It's not like I got the whole nine-yards the last time I was here."

I was so hoping she would ask. It's one of my favorite parts: the explanation of what is.

What's to come.

I spread my arms. "Welcome to the mirror world, darling. The thing that hides behind all reflections."

She just sits there. Unimpressed.

"This is the part where you ask *how*," I supply helpfully.

She clenches her jaw.

"I'll give you a hint: Man was never made to see his own reflection." I smirk. "And for that matter, neither was Woman."

I reach forward and a bowl of glittering sugar cubes unfolds near the teakettle as I pluck one from the top. I drop it into my cup with a plunk.

"Back when the world was new, people had to kneel to see themselves. They had to catch their reflections in ponds and puddles. Someone even summed it up in a neat little quote, once: Pessoa, I think his name was. Fernando."

A dainty spoon materializes between my fingers and clinks against the inner edges of the teacup as I stir.

"But mankind got greedy, as they are hardwired to do, and created clearer and sharper reflectors. They looked into them longer and longer—became obsessed with their own sense of self. It evolved into a human habit—and splintered a world behind their reflections."

I've become lost in my own exposition. I register the blankness of Maia's face with disappointment.

"Are you quite finished?" she asks.

I get the distinct feeling she's mocking me somehow.

I set my teacup back on its crystal saucer. "I remember your lack of flair. How boring."

"You're the one in a black suit," she murmurs. "Can't get more boring than that."

A flare of anger licks up my spine at her petulance. "Oh …" My grin is wider and sharper than it should be. "You're much braver than you were seven years ago."

"I was a *kid*."

I shrug. "I have something to show you."

A flicker of excitement lights up my fingertips as I stand, like a child eager to show off their toys. I pointedly ignore the fact that Maia might not be around long enough to truly enjoy what I show her as I motion for her to follow.

Invisible hands push her back into the chair when she begins to stand.

The chair raises from the floor instead and follows me as though on a leash.

"Play *nice*, remember?" I say over my shoulder.

Her glare could sheer steel.

As an afterthought, I step back to grab my tea and saucer from the table. Sip it as I walk.

One of the walls peels away to reveal a grand balcony. I drop Maia's chair carelessly to its surface.

She scowls up at me.

Below us, the true form of the mirror world is endless—unfathomable to a human mind even with its 100 trillion neural connections.

But take that human mind and place it here: In a world that fractures it. Reflects it. Fractals it.

You see why humans can't stand up to the mirror's pressure?

The surface below us is sleek. Black. Amaranthine and infinite.

Its creatures wander the surface, mindless in their drifting, countless in their numbers. They wear the shapes of mankind, but not the expressions. Not the individualities.

Systematic and uniform, they are blank slates of canvas for the mirror to use as it sees fit.

It is the creator.

And I, the curator.

"Why are you showing me this?" Maia's voice breaks my admiration of the mirror's creations. She's looking up at me like I'm mad for marveling at my own home.

I raise my cup to my mouth and hesitate. "What do they look like to you?"

Maia gestures as though it should be obvious. "People."

I frown into my tea. "Well … that says something deep, doesn't it?" I murmur.

"Explain."

"The mirror is a reflector, and only that. Without me, it can only show you what you fear most. So these are, in essence …"

"Reflections."

I giggle. "Ah, she learns."

"What do they look like to you?"

I raise a brow, touched by the fact that she even cares. "I can make them look like anything. In fact, I'm sure you'll become very familiar with my work shortly." I grin, unable to help myself. "But, when I first arrived, they looked like monsters. Boogie men and creatures from the closet and nightmares in general." I shrug. "You know: a typical 6-year-old's horrors."

She frowns as the calculation goes through her head. "You were only six?"

"And I've been here ever since," I say proudly.

She studies me for an uncomfortably long moment. "That explains the tea party and your lacking knowledge of social cues."

Her wit can cut when she means it to.

I take in her folded arms and lowered brow and the way she puts the full weight of her back against the chair.

Her disinterest is as clear as it's insulting.

"How old are you?" she asks bluntly.

Her question sparks an uncomfortable string of memories:

I remember the cold stone of the castle hallways, the ring of the blacksmith's anvil in the marketplace, the tart zing of the custard I was never allowed to eat, the smell of the straw that made up my bed.

I remember my mother.

A heavy-set, bitter woman with fingerprints dotting her apron no matter how many times she washed it and a deep scowl between her eyes no matter what I did.

I sip from my tea and peer at Maia over the rim. "A lady never shares her age."

"You could just say you don't remember."

My teacup clatters a little too hard onto its saucer. "Rather like I *chose* to forget."

"Sure." She watches the creatures wander below a moment longer. "Where do they come from?"

"They're echoes: the lost reflections of anyone who's ever looked into a mirror with a negative thought. In layman's terms: a person loses a piece of themselves every time they do that, and—in case you're not following along—it ends up here. Quite poetic, really."

I turn my attention from Maia to the creatures, watching them mindlessly drift by each other like people passing on the streets.

It's a thing I've done since I was young—separate and yet a part of them.

"They might not seem all that grand in their purest form, but they were once very human. Many can even split from the same person—one for every heinous thought that races through their head as they look into the mirror. And that isn't even the greatest part: these that you see here are very little of what exists in this world.

"Too many people are on the brink of a secret madness, a virus as old as humankind: Insecurity. It's what convinces people they're too much. And yet, never enough. They're too weird, too ugly, too large, too curious, too uncontrolled, too emotional, too messy, too dark, too, too, too, too, too … much. That's what it comes down to, really. They're too much.

"So that's what they become. One glance in a mirror with one of those nasty, messy thoughts, and a tiny particle of themselves ends up here and fractures—

the mirror world reflects that same rotten thought a thousandfold—until the world itself is altered. An ever-changing mass of *too much*."

I glance down at her, trying to gauge her reaction to all of this.

Some people cry. Some tremble in fear.

Some can feel the mirror's subtle splintering into their mind, and they panic before I even get the chance to showcase the horror and beauty of this place.

Maia's face is the same carefully blank expression she's had since she entered, so entirely different from her earlier panic that it throws me each time I see it.

I lead her back to the tea table.

"Is it sentient? The mirror?"

I drop her chair back into place and sit across from her, this time the proper way. "Not entirely."

She raises a brow for me to go on and I look pointedly at her untouched cup of tea.

Her lips form a thin line. "Is it poisoned?"

"It wouldn't do me much good if it was, would it?"

A brief pause passes before she pinches the handle of the dainty mug between her fingertips and takes a tiny sip. I can't tell if she slurps it for my sake or because she's a sloppy drinker.

Only after she swallows do I speak:

"It's *old*," I answer. "Far older than me."

I sip from my own tea. "I don't believe even the mirror itself knows how it came into being. It simply *Wasn't* one day, and then it *Was*. In the years since its creation, it's absorbed all human knowledge and error. Their negative thoughts are the creatures that welcomed you seven years ago. And when someone dares to break the very thing their species created, the mirror reaches out and takes them for itself. That's all a mirror can do, really: take. It reflects only a superficial image. Everything else is absorbed."

She chews on the inside of her cheek. "Where are my friends?" she says finally.

I lean against the back of the chair and inspect my nails. "How would I know?"

"Let them go."

I click my tongue. "Such a demanding little thing. Might I remind you that this is my *home*. You can't come barging into a lady's home making demands."

"Let. Them. Go."

"Mmm …" I raise the teacup to my lips and hum around my tea. "Mmhmm, see, I just don't understand why you think I can do that."

Her frustration pulls tight—I can feel it even with the gateway so quiet between us. "Cryptic villains are really out of style, you know," she says through her teeth. "Your little minions follow your every move, which means you're obviously in charge here."

The word halts my amusement in its tracks.

Minion is an ugly term, synonymous with bootlicker, doormat, lackey.

The mirror's creatures may follow my every order—they may be nothing more than constructs of thought that I can weave to my every purpose—but to call them *minions* is to call *me* unprincipled and dishonorable.

I prefer the term *liberator.*

She makes a noise at the back of her throat when I don't answer. "Why am I here?"

"Your seven years are over. Surely you made that connection from the common myth."

"No. Why am I *here*, sitting at your stupid tea party? You want me to finish our game?" she guesses. "You're holding my friends as prizes? Do I win one back each time I find you?" There's an unwelcome sarcastic, angry tone in her voice.

"Oh, I won't be the one hiding. You didn't find me last time we played; why would you care to find me now?"

Her eyes widen when she realizes my meaning. "Where are they? What have you done with them?"

"The rules of the game are simple, Maia: *You* find your friends, and *I'll* let them go."

She hesitates. "That's it? The only thing I have to do is find them?"

"I wasn't finished. You must also *play* the game."

She looks at me like I'm daft.

"Don't play coy with me. I know you took a piece of this place when you escaped. I know you've felt its power squirming around beneath your skin for the past seven years. I've grown bored of opponents who dissolve to their fear so quickly, and I want someone to *play* with me. I'll even make you a deal: find all of your friends before sunrise, and I won't even return for them in seven years."

"Why let us go at all?"

"You misunderstand. I'll let your friends go, yes, but *you* are a thing the mirror has had and lost, and it will not lose you again."

She's quiet, contemplative. A string of her earlier fear coils through the gateway between us like smoke, slow and unhurried.

She knew she wouldn't be going home before she stepped through the frame.

"Better hurry—" I whisper.

The tearoom shimmers around us like a wire on the fritz and unwinds piece by piece.

Maia's chair lifts her to a standing position before it, too, dissolves.

A set of seven dark, mirrored steps extends upward from her feet, set into a narrow stairwell as I fade into the shadows.

"Time is something of a fluid subject here, and you're already running out of it."

At the top of the stairs is a blank black door.

Above it, a single, buzzing, neon pink sign:

PLAYROOM

"Dolls? Seriously?"

I feel the memory go through Maia's mind like a quick breeze:

She sat with Rylee and June late one Halloween night, trading scary stories and fears by flashlight.

"Dolls," Rylee said when it was her turn.

"Dolls? Seriously?" June laughed.

"Maybe. Probably?" Rylee rolled her eyes and smacked June's knee. "Stop looking at me like that! My grandma has this creepy doll that always like, watches over the playroom and—"

June teased her relentlessly for weeks afterward.

I remember it as well as Maia does.

She looks up at the sign from the bottom of the stairs.

"Rylee first, then," she whispers to herself.

SEVEN

Don't Cut the Strings

The door creaks open to reveal the same sleek, empty surface we saw from the balcony.

Maia hesitates in the threshold, eyes darting back and forth, a furrow between her brows as though expecting to see something that just isn't there.

"Rylee?" she whispers.

The echo bounces around a few moments before returning. Before the chime of a music box fills the space, steadily growing louder.

Voices drift from somewhere unseen, listless and multidirectional.

Come and play, they say.
Come and play, they say.
Come and play, they say.

Maia steps through the door and it dissolves behind her. She is the only speck of dust on a vast glass table.

"*Rylee.*" Her whisper is louder this time, harsher.

She wanders the empty space until she walks into something.

She flinches.

There's the thunk of a stage light turning on.

It crowns the oversized doll in brilliant pink as the thing wobbles on one of its pointed toes, teeters, tips, and shatters across the floor.

The thunk thunk thunk of more lights sound, illuminating an innumerable and wonderfully diversified crowd of them.

They stipple the mirror world like stars, all with their own beam to light their silhouettes from above.

The first puppet drops right in front of her.

She stumbles backward, trips over her own feet into a group of them. They sway and knock together, wood clattering like a discordant windchime.

She spins in a slow circle and is met in each direction with a different face. A different material. Different clothing.

But all the same type of toy.

Some wear dresses, their hair coiffed and perfect. Others wear undergarments as though their owners haven't dressed them yet.

Their rosy cheeks and wide, unblinking eyes give the illusion of innocence, whether their frozen faces are smiling or shaped into a pout or devoid of expression altogether.

And they all move in languorously eerie ways:

Life-sized artist mannequins turn their blank wooden heads this way and that. Glass ballerinas pirouette on crystal pedestals to the music box's tune. Marionettes in ornate reds and greens and blues swing from strings that stretch far into the darkness above. Vintage baby dolls blink slowly, neon light gleaming in their glass eyes.

Joints tink and clack.

The porcelain creatures sound like a cupboard full of china, the wooden ones like a bucket full of sticks. And though not all of them are tied up with strings, their languid actions are all controlled by a puppeteer.

Me, thank you very much.

All together, they create a forest of porcelain and wood and fine china.

Maia takes a deep breath and weaves through them. Drags her feet in caution, stepping lightly, taking care not to stray too near to them.

She does a double take as she passes one of the ballerinas. Squints at its face.

As if an idea occurs to her, she picks up her pace, studying every face she passes.

Large eyes, painted mouths, wooden noses, porcelain cheeks.

Her speed increases each time it isn't Rylee staring back.

I move her around as Maia seeks.

She looks at Rylee three separate times before recognition finally hits.

Rylee dances with chilling, unhurried precision:

Fingers stiff and graceful, neck lengthened like a swan, eyes wide and unblinking.

The hem of her soft pink frock brushes her shins, rippling like it's caught in a current. Her pointed toes are laced into shoes. Golden hair cascades down her back in ripples, moving quite the same as the hem of her gown.

Even the gentlest movements splinter her skin, the hairline fractures barely visible against the pale white.

She really is a lovely creation.

I've outdone myself.

Rylee spins into a grand jeté, the movement taking a full nineteen seconds.

Maia's mouth parts in shock and maybe a little bit of awe as she follows beside her.

"Rylee?"

Rylee's doll eyes stare straight ahead, pupils a flat, expressionless black. She moves with the grace of smoke. The elusiveness of mist.

Maia gazes around helplessly, her uncertainty plain. Surely when I suggested hide-and-seek, she wasn't expecting her friends to *become* the things that hid them.

What a twist.

A groan snaps through the floor, like the unstable surface of a frozen lake, and she instinctively throws her arms out to her sides, fingers splayed in surprise, knees bent.

She looks down at her feet.

And gets her mouth open to scream just as the floor shatters out from beneath her.

I pull up a velvet chaise lounge at the bottom of her trajectory and hang cords above my head as she falls, the twitch of my fingers tying both ends to the blackness above so they hang in loops.

She'll need something to catch her, after all.

I sink into the plush couch and wait.

And wait.

And wait.

I let her fall for a few more moments.

Her mouth is open in a silent scream. Wind rushes past so fast it tumbles her head over toes.

I can tell when she spots the tangle of strings, because she does finally make a noise: a breathless gasp that cuts short when her ankle catches on one of the cords.

She launches forward.

Her elbow snags on another, and like a frisbee catching on tree branches in its downward path, she's tossed like a rag doll.

There's a brief, startling moment when I wonder if she might not stop at all.

Finally, she pitches forward, belly down, and lands at the base of the bottommost loop.

The cord stops her so abruptly her body folds in half around it.

Her forehead narrowly avoids cracking into her shins.

I'll admit, I didn't mean for it to be *that* hard of a landing.

It's several long, choking moments before she finally inhales—a raw, scraping thing. It ends in a fit of coughing. She dry heaves like she might vomit.

I stand and scooch my chaise back a bit before sitting down again.

The sound snaps her gaze to me.

I sip from the tea I never got to finish and glance up at her. My drink is warm despite the coldness of her stare.

"*You*—" she wheezes. "You said—"

"Take your time."

She groans as she wriggles her weight around. Pushes at the length of cord to scoot it from her stomach to her chest until she dangles by her underarms. Then her hands.

She drops to the floor and crumples, arms crossed over her aching belly. Another fit of coughing takes her. She glowers at me. "You *said*—"

The floor shatters, and I break apart with it, laughing.

She screams this time.

The plunge into darkness is brief, and instead of Maia alone, colossal marionettes and puppets drop with her. She is roughly the size of their hands, the width of their foreheads, the thickness of their strings.

A clatter sounds as they all catch tension, strings pulling taut to knock them together.

Maia kicks uselessly among them, legs flailing above the new ground. Her own strings cut into her armpits—I can almost feel the chafe from here.

"You said my only task was to *find* them—" she snarls.

I assemble myself into a thing the size of the puppets swaying around us. Maia's entire body is as big as my nose. I stare down the length of it at her.

"Uh, *yeah* …?"

I shrink to match her size and push at her foot that dangles just above my head. She kicks out and nearly cracks several of my fingers. I frown up at her. "So why are we still here?"

"You're asking *me?*" She squirms against the pull of the ropes, which only tightens them around her shoulders.

I roll my eyes. "Perhaps I was unclear about your role earlier: you're supposed to be *playing* the game."

Maia stops squirming. "I am!"

I raise a dubious brow. "You're not doing very well."

"I found her, didn't I?"

I make a show of looking around. A smirk twists up the corner of my mouth. "Did you?"

"I *found—*"

I slice a hand through the air and snap every string.

Maia's scream is lost to the air racing by.

She lands on her feet this time, stringless. Detached. She seems almost as impressed by this fact as she is frustrated by the sheer number of creatures that surround her.

They hang from trusses, litter the floor—tiny trinkets and massive things and every conceivable size between.

Velvet curtains drop from above, edges brushing the floor.

"Rylee!" Maia calls, apparently no longer concerned with caution.

She shoves a path through the mirror's creatures, checking every face. She picks them off the ground, climbs the arms of those large as houses.

"Rylee!"

A glimmer of golden hair catches a passing neon streak and Maia breaks into a run, heedless of the destruction she leaves in her wake:

Shattered porcelain figures, wooden trinkets with their limbs all askew, strings hopelessly tangled as her path sends them swinging.

Maia catches hold of her friend as the girl rotates in a slow pirouette, stopping her movement.

"Rylee," Maia pants.

She clamps her hands onto Rylee's shoulders so tightly I expect to see hairline fissures crack across porcelain skin.

"*Hey.*" She shakes Rylee like she expects the jarring sensation to shake the girl back to herself.

As if it would be so simple.

"Rylee, I don't … I don't know how to fix this."

She shakes her again.

"*Rylee!*"

Maia curses under her breath, a habit that's progressively developed since she met June.

She looks around.

"*Hey.*" Her demand is sharp enough to tell exactly who it's aimed at.

I step from the shadows. "You rang?"

"You said"—she stops, swallows, tries to catch her breath—"*finding* them was the only task."

She hardly flinches as I rest an elbow on Rylee's cold shoulder and lean against the doll.

Maia doesn't so much as look at me: her eyes stay glued to Rylee's face, hardly blinking. She hardly *breathes*, as though one wrong move could fracture the entire moment—send her careening into darkness again.

It could, after all.

I adjust my glasses. "You can't possibly think to send her home like this, though, can you?" I flick an imaginary speck of dust from the tip of Rylee's upturned nose and wipe my hand on my lapel. "What would poor Mrs. Monroe think? Teddy would never speak to you again. And don't think I don't know about that little candle you still hold for him. Honestly, don't you think it's time to give that up? He's in college now—"

"You said finding them was the *only* task," she repeats it like a broken record, like it's the only thing her flustered mind can generate to say.

Her gaze bores into Rylee's face as though she can reach into her friend's mind and pull her out through sheer willpower alone.

Her fingers squeeze tighter on Rylee's shoulders like she can anchor her with whatever physical strength a 16-year-old girl has to her advantage.

There's something more, though, hidden beneath Maia's will: an electric current that buzzes in the air around her.

She doesn't seem to recognize the taste of her own power.

"I also said you must *play the game*. Maybe you didn't notice, but it seems rather apparent that the game is playing *you*."

She stares daggers at Rylee but speaks to me: "I don't *understand*."

"I'll give you a hint, then, in simple terms that you can chew slowly: That piece of the mirror you stole gives you the same power as I. You can play this game as well as I can … *if* you'd only stop fighting the mirror."

"Even if I could do something like that, I don't know *how*—"

"You'd better figure it out." I take my leaning arm off Rylee's shoulder and straighten my posture.

"Oh, and you'd better get to her before *they* do."

I pop out of sight with a crack.

Maia closes her eyes, takes a deep breath.

When she opens them again, that curious violet ring around her pupils is a shade brighter. Through the gateway between us, I catch a peculiar echo—a straining in her core as she tries to reach into Rylee's mind and pull her from her reverie.

If I wasn't so curious to see what she'll do when she fails, I would just pop back and tell her:

Only the mirror can reach into minds.

I can alter the reality, puppet the characters, but only *it* can make them believe.

"Rylee."

Maia's voice is the calm cobalt of ocean water before a storm.

Rylee's doll eyes stare straight ahead, gaze connected with Maia's and yet far from it.

"*Rylee.*"

A ripple rolls through the calm ocean of Maia's voice in the form of a quiver.

There's a noise, then—

Faint, but growing steadily louder.

A snapping of sorts, like a bridge cable pulled too taut.

Maia looks up, gaze zeroing in on the marionette strings that disappear into the darkness above.

One tightens as she watches, then breaks. The end flutters down from somewhere unseen, and beneath it—somewhere in the outer reaches of the crowd of creatures—is an outbreak of motion, like something has been cut loose.

Maia tightens her grip on Rylee until her knuckles turn white. "*Rylee.*"

Another string snaps.

Another.

Another.

"Rylee, snap out of it."

The click of joints grows in volume, the horde pushing in at Maia and Rylee in the center.

Another.

Another.

"Look at me—"

Another.

"*Please!*" Maia looks around wildly.

The creatures rush them, a tidal wave of clinking joints and painted mouths.

Maia's desperation gets the better of her.

She slaps Rylee across the face so hard the girl stumbles.

It surprises such a harsh laugh out of me that Rylee's strings slip through my fingers.

She gasps like a drowning man.

The creatures halt their attack.

I suppose Maia has won this round, in a way.

The dolls' rigid fingers wipe at their eyes, sorry to see Rylee go.

They wave stiffly before crumbling away.

EIGHT

Running Out of Time

Rylee blinks like she's forgotten how to. Looks around like a newborn discovering their capacity for sight.

Those doll eyes really are a pain.

She finally focuses on Maia, and the shock registers in her body like hot water, melting away the stiffness of porcelain, the cold of lifelessness. Her mouth opens and closes a few times before she can speak. "Maia? How are you—how are you here?"

"I came to find you." Maia looks around and behind Rylee, and I think I'll never tire of her naive hope of finding her friends in plain sight. "Where are the others?"

Rylee rubs at her cheek, the skin already red and swelling. "That hurt."

Maia grabs her shoulders again. "Rylee, *where are the others?*"

"I don't know. What's going on?"

"The *mirror*, that's what's going on!" Maia says this as though Rylee should know. As though Rylee's small human brain has ever even attempted to wrap itself around the idea of such a place as this.

Maia grabs her hand and begins to tug Rylee behind. "C'mon, we've got to find them."

She stops suddenly. Softens. I feel her remember her own terror at this place.

"Hey, but listen—" She pulls Rylee into a quick, crushing hug, and a sharp spike of jealousy digs into my spine. "I'm really glad you're okay."

Maia's back to business like the flip of a switch, grabbing at Rylee's hand again. "She told me if I find you all before sunrise, she'd let you go, but she's going to make it harder every time, so—"

"She?"

Maia pauses. "There's this … woman here. Or … not a woman? Maybe she's even part of the mirror itself." At Rylee's confused look, Maia elaborates: "Noire's in charge of all this."

My heartbeat stalls.

I don't remember ever telling her my name. Granted, she could merely remember it from her first visit but—

Allow me to check something really quick.

. . .

No. She never knew it, even then.

Perhaps the mirror is getting to her quicker than I anticipated—spilling its secrets inside to pull out her own.

"She controls everything here?" Rylee asks.

Maia nods solemnly. "Everything, Ry, so we gotta be careful. Don't do anything you'd usually do." She leaves again only to turn around when she realizes Rylee isn't following her.

Rylee is rooted in place, lost. Gaze flicking around as though she's seeing everything for the first time.

"Rylee."

"I don't believe this. I'm dreaming, right? If I just pinch myself hard enough—"

Maia leaps in to grab her hand. "You're not dreaming. And we're running out of time."

Again, she begins pulling Rylee after her— "*C'mon*, Ry, we gotta go."

And again, Rylee is resistant.

"I think I need to sit down—just for a minute, Mai."

Maia finally takes a good look at her friend. "Okay …" She glances around as though trying to see a way out of this necessary pause, but finally relents. "Okay, yeah. Just for a minute."

Rylee sinks to the floor, and I can almost see the gears turning in her brain as she tries to make sense of any of this. "So, Lucy and June are … probably like I was? Trapped in this place?"

"Yes." Maia laughs breathlessly, still flighty.

I don't blame her. If I were up against time in a race to find my friends in a world I didn't understand, I'd be impetuous too.

If I *had* friends. And if I cared for them at all.

"Why?" Rylee asks.

"She's hiding you guys from me. Like some messed up version of hide-and-seek. She keeps saying she wants me to 'play' her game. Emphasis on the *play*."

"Where are we? You said"—Rylee frowns—"the mirror? What mirror?"

"Your mom's antique one. In the attic, remember? You guys broke it. It took you inside. That's where we are now."

For all her intelligence, Rylee looks like a child trying to grasp the concept of molecular physics.

"C'mon, Ry," Maia says softly. "You're the one who still wants to believe in dragons and castles and fairytale worlds."

Rylee looks up, brows drawn together. "This isn't a fairytale, Maia. This is *real.* And terrifying." She looks down at her hands, as though ashamed of her fear.

Or perhaps she remembers the feel of her porcelain skin.

"You remember that doll my grandma had that I always hated?"

Maia sits beside Rylee. "Yeah. Yeah, I do. Noire is really great at exploiting people's fears …"

Again, my name out of her mouth triggers in me a fight or flight response I'd never thought to anticipate.

"How do you know all this?" Rylee asks.

When Maia doesn't respond, she prompts: "Maia?"

"We gotta get June and Lucy, Rylee. We're running out of time."

Rylee sighs and nods. "All right. Let's go."

NINE

The Cave

The further they walk, the more uneven the ground becomes. A distant sound of dripping water echoes through the space.

The edges of the mirror world shrink around them, slowly taking on textures and generating the rough edge of rock.

Rylee trails a hand along the nearest section, fingers stumbling over the dips and peaks and crags. "How does this work?" Her voice is quiet, awed.

For the moment, her fear seems to have hidden behind her curiosity, peaking around its shoulders only enough to remind her not to talk too loud.

"Noire controls—"

"Everything. You said. But how?" The wall shifts beneath her fingertips and she snaps her hand back. "And *why?*"

Maia stares straight ahead, as though refusing to acknowledge the mirror world—or me—any more than necessary.

A high ceiling finally comes into view, gradually sloping lower as the girls continue walking.

The air turns damp.

"I keep thinking about what you said back there," Rylee starts.

"Which part?"

"All of it. That Noire controls everything and not to do anything we'd usually do and all that. Oh, and you never actually answered my question."

Maia's eyes track the shifting of the mirror's edges around her, the glimmers of light catching on the rock's craggy surface.

"*Maia*," Rylee prompts.

"Which question?"

Maia's emotions aren't strong enough for me to feel even the faintest suggestion of them just now, but I know her well enough to sense when she's stalling.

"How do you know all of this? And another question … how did you get here in the first place? If we're really inside the mirror"—she makes a face like a scientist exploring the possibility of magic—"then how are *you* here? You weren't even there when it broke."

"I left my phone," Maia lies. "I came back to get it. You were all gone."

Blue light begins to highlight the moisture clinging to the walls, dripping in a steady cadence from sharp stalactites. The rest of the cave glows with an eerie green hue, barely bright enough to reveal the shape of the ground they walk on.

Rylee watches her feet, stepping much more carefully than Maia.

"So you just … assumed we were in the mirror? How did you figure that out? Did you stick your hand through the empty frame? Accidentally fall into it? Did those things come out and get you? And how would you even know to *think* that the broken mirror had anything to do with us being gone? What if we were all just … in Teddy's room messing around with his stuff or something?"

"Rylee …"

"You've been here before, haven't you?"

It's only because she's looking at Maia now that she can see the brief flicker of guilt that crosses Maia's expression.

"You *have.*"

Maia picks up her pace. Not enough to be noticeable, but enough to distance herself a few inches from Rylee.

"So, like … when? And how? And why didn't you tell any of us?"

Maia picks up her pace again. This time it *is* noticeable, and Rylee lengthens her stride to catch up.

"Is this why you have nightmares? Why you won't ever stay for sleepovers? Is this why you always get weird when we hang out in the attic and why there's no mirror in your bathroom?"

"Enough, Ry."

"No, I need to know." Rylee's gentle demeanor shifts, takes on an incontestable edge—she speaks mildly, like a mother to her daughter, but her tone no longer brokers room for argument. "Maybe I can understand why you didn't say anything before—it didn't really matter. But we're all in this together now. You, me, June, Lucy—"

Maia sighs. "I need your help."

I marvel at the tiny deviation in her mood. It's as if she knows which of Rylee's strings to pull to change the subject—shift the topic of conversation away from herself and focus instead on Rylee's need to help.

It does the trick, and Rylee softens. Her brows draw together with worry again instead of demand. "With what?"

"Getting Lucy and June out."

Rylee slows, falls behind. "Why? What about you?"

"It's nothing," Maia says too quickly. She amends when Rylee catches back up: "Two is always better than one, right? I can't do this all on my own."

Rylee bites at her bottom lip, an old habit showing its face. "Okay," she agrees. "But when we get home, I want to know everything."

"You will—"

Maia throws out an arm, stopping Rylee an inch away from the sheer drop below.

"Whoa," Rylee whispers.

The sound echoes throughout the cavern, wide as a crater and twice as deep. The roof of the void is too high to be found.

"Thanks," she says breathlessly.

"Lucy's afraid of snakes, right?"

"Yeah, why?"

Maia points to the steel-blue lake at the bottom of the chasm, the surface lacerated by serpentine bodies.

"Because I think we'll find her next."

TEN
Basilisk

"You think Lucy's in *that?*" Rylee's eyes are wide, the whites reflecting the green light.

Maia takes a deep breath. "Or somewhere nearby." She runs a hand through her hair, fingers tangling. She pulls the elastic off her wrist and flips her head upside down.

"You're not seriously going in there—"

Maia speaks as she ties her hair into a bun: "If it were you, you'd want someone to come get you, right?"

Rylee wrings her hands together so hard her knuckles turn white.

Maia stands up straight.

"Yeah … okay." Rylee crouches to untie her pointe shoes.

Maia stiffens. "You can't come."

Rylee's fingers pause. She looks up at Maia. "Why not?"

Maia hesitates, and I can almost feel her reasoning through the thing that binds us:

Because the mirror only wants me. Because I don't trust it to let you go if it traps you again.

"Just … stay here, okay? It's not a good idea for both of us to go in. What if something happens?"

Rylee stands and puts her hands on her hips. "Yeah, Maia, what if something happens? To *you?* Those things could be poisonous. They could have fangs longer than your arm— I can't even tell how *big* they are, it's such a long drop. You could break your neck just by hitting the water—"

"I can't play Noire's stupid game if I'm dead."

Rylee bites her lip again. "I'll stay here," she finally relents.

Maia slips off her sneakers and tosses her socks over the top. She looks down at herself like she's wondering if there's anything else she should take off.

Rylee folds her arms. "But if you're underwater for more than a minute, I'm coming in after you. At least yell at me every once in a while so I know you're still alive."

A shadow of uncertainty passes over Maia's face. There was a time—before she knew about this world—when her worst fears were drowning and quicksand.

"Yeah." She shakes her nerves out through her hands. "Good plan."

She doesn't allow herself a moment to reconsider and leaps as far out from the cliffside as she can.

Her arms pinwheel as she drops. She clenches her teeth so hard a vein stands out in her forehead, but a scream still escapes at the last second.

It's cut short as she breaks the chilly surface, bubbles exploding behind her as she cuts through like a torpedo. She kicks upward before her momentum even slows.

She breaks the surface and coughs up a lungful of fluid. Not quite slimy, but not as thin a liquid as water, either.

"Glad to know you're still alive," Rylee's voice echoes down the cavern walls.

"Keep an eye out!" Maia calls back, treading water. "Just in case Lucy's out there somewhere."

"Got it!"

Maia pulls in a breath like a captain going down with their ship and ducks under.

Slithering bodies disturb the lake around her. In some places, they're so thickly tangled she has to stick a hand through—nudge the knot apart enough to pass.

She sticks to the surface at first, skimming the murky expanse below for any sign of Lucy.

The serpents are so black they suck in the light around them. The tiniest ones are the diameter of her pinky and barely five times its length. The largest are as big around as her bicep.

She counts to 58 in her head each time she goes under; I can hear the echo of her timekeeping in my own head. She does it to keep herself calm, like when she counts to ten.

But also because Rylee's surely counting as well and wouldn't hesitate to make good on her word.

Maia's head breaks the surface, and she sucks in a breath as a viper slides along the back of her arm, its pace languid.

"I'm up," she calls.

The monstrous cavern amplifies their voices so well they can hear each other without yelling.

Rylee's reply drifts from above: "Anything?"

"No. You?"

"No."

Maia curses.

"I heard that." A pause. And then: "June would be proud."

"I gotta go deeper, Ry."

"Fine: two minutes."

Just before Maia ducks under, Rylee murmurs, "Guess it's a good thing you're a swimmer …"

Maia dives straight down this time, kicking hard, paddling harder. The serpents get longer, thicker.

At 53 seconds she turns back, having reached an impassable layer of basilisks as big around as she.

"Anything?" she calls to Rylee.

"No."

Maia goes back under.

67 seconds.

72.

81.

Her eyes are wide as she navigates the waters, kicking through creatures more monstrous the deeper she goes, but her expression isn't one of fear. She gazes around in what looks like wonder. Awe.

What I wouldn't give to know her true thoughts just now.

She turns back at 88 seconds.

She breaks the surface, and Rylee is already screaming her name.

Maia fills her lungs with much-needed air. "I'm up, I'm up!"

This time it's Rylee who curses.

"*Language*," Maia says.

"Bite me."

It's the most attitude Rylee's ever given to anyone.

Despite herself, Maia laughs.

It tapers away quickly.

"Anything?" she asks, suddenly somber.

Rylee's pause says everything it needs to.

"I'm going back down, no counting this time. I think we've established that these things are harmle—"

A heavy tail wraps around her waist and *yanks*.

Her open mouth fills with water.

The surface of the lake erupts in churning whitewater, basilisks and vipers in bedlam, cutting through the water like scythes.

Maia pushes against the coiled snake around her middle, legs kicking wildly, desperately, hopelessly.

On the cliff face, Rylee screams: "*Maia!*"

I unfold stairs from the cavern wall to her left and Rylee takes them without hesitation, running the perimeter of the chasm a time and a half before the spiral finally reaches the bottom.

She lurches to her hands and knees, skinning them on the rock, and leans over to peer into the churning surface.

It boils like a cauldron, nothing visible but scales.

"*Maia!*" she screams again.

The creature wraps tighter around Maia's waist, likely crushing a few ribs. I ease the pressure a bit.

I want to *play* with my toys, not break them.

She pushes against the snake with all the effort she has left and slips its hold—claws her way back to the surface.

A serpent cuts into her path from the right, knocking her aside so hard the current rolls her.

Another hits her in the back.

She kicks wildly. The serpents' thrashing tumbles her like a washing machine.

Her chest hitches with the remnants of her air.

It hitches again when she glimpses the serpent that has Lucy's eyes.

A basilisk twice as thick as Maia's body hits her head-on, expelling any oxygen she's managed to hold on to. Its momentum folds her over the tip of its nose. She claws at its eyes as it swims down

down

do

wn

d

o

w

n

d

o

w

n

Maia's fight loses momentum until her hands barely drift along its scales.

Her neck lolls forward with the current rushing past. Her head bows until it rests between the snake's eyes.

The serpent changes direction, and the shift knocks her from its snout.

She drifts amid the chaos, the only serene thing in the lake.

I'm on the verge of wondering if I've made a mistake—if perhaps she isn't the opponent I thought she would be—when her body spasms.

And like a detonation beneath the water, the shock wave ripples from her to the surface.

To the shore, where it soaks Rylee's frock to the waist.

Deep in the abyss, Maia takes a breath.

And now …

Now, we're playing.

In the wake of the shock wave, the lake's composition changes to a thing her lungs can process. Clarity follows the ripple outward, dissipating the murkiness. Every serpent but one falls still.

Perfluorocarbon: a crystal clear, breathable liquid.

It's not knowledge she would have without the mirror. It's not anything she would have learned in school.

It's *impressive.*

Imagine what she might be capable of when she knows what she's doing.

Her body spasms again.

She takes a second breath, coughs.

Drags in a third, coughs.

A fourth breath.

A fifth.

Her eyes are twin pools of violet fire when she opens them.

She searches the twisted bodies between her and the surface—only one of them still moves.

She pushes off the silty bottom and kicks upward until she's close enough.

And then she strikes the serpent in what you could call a chest—palm flat, arm locked—and the creature dissipates as it expels Lucy backward.

I frown with my mouth and my brow, a feeling in the back of my mind like I'm missing something.

Lucy drifts upward as the remaining serpents disintegrate downward.

Maia grabs her beneath the arms, prepares to pull her to the surface.

But I drain the liquid.

I can be merciful, you see:

After all, her survival instinct gave her the key to unlock her power.

And in the next round, I'll make her use it.

Maia and Lucy lower softly into the silt.

"Maia?" Rylee's voice is thin with distance. She's a small, pink figure at the edge of a 500-foot crater. Maia and Lucy are two small figures at the bottom.

"Maia!" Rylee grips the edge and scales the pit's curved wall. She half-runs, half-slides through fading scree and talus, and by the time she reaches the bottom, the mirror world is iridescent black again: reset and ready for another round.

Maia chokes and sputters, her lungs making yet another switch between liquid and air.

She bends over her knees to shake Lucy. "Lucy? Hey, Lucy. Look at me."

Rylee stands over Maia's shoulder. The mud on her pointe shoes peels away and disappears. "Is she …"

"She's fine." It seems to me that Maia says this more for her own sake than Rylee's. "She has to be."

I materialize with a slow clap. Overrated, but it's what the moment calls for. "*There* she is: our hero Maia."

I stand near Rylee, and Rylee steps away.

"Two out of three already, Hartley? I'm impressed." My tone is teasing, but I can't keep the awe from my voice. I click my tongue. "I suppose I'll have to make the next round a bit more difficult."

Maia is eerily still.

Her gaze is pinned on Lucy, but the anger in her shoulders is a blade directed at me.

"*Don't.*"

Lucy coughs, choking up fluid in spurts. "Maia?" she croaks. "Rylee?" She looks between them before noticing me. "What's going on?"

"Hi there." I smile warmly, to make her feel welcome.

"*Why are you here,*" Maia demands between her teeth. She stares daggers at the non-floor as if it would kill her to look at me. "The game isn't over yet."

"Game?" Lucy asks.

"Give me the next round," Maia commands.

"No."

"Maia …" Rylee cautions at the look in my eyes. Her gaze ricochets between Maia and me.

"You're not even playing."

Now Maia looks at me, and her eyes glow with fury.

The violet ring has faded in brightness, but grows wider still.

"I *am* playing," she says. "I'm finding them, isn't that what you want?"

"What I want"—I step so close it forces her to look straight up at me—"is for you to *play the game.*"

"I—"

"*No*, you're not. The game is playing you."

Maia squares her jaw as she fully understands my meaning. It's no fun playing with a partner who won't countermove. It's too easy.

"*Play*, Maia. Play with me."

"You almost killed me just now. I'm *done*. Give me June," she seethes.

I smile,

and a crack of thunder bursts through the mirror world, so loud several of the frames in the Monroe house vibrate:

Mrs. Monroe's silhouette is backlit by her fridge as she gets a late-night drink.

She glances at the mirror in the entryway off the kitchen. Wanders over and pokes at the bottom left corner, as though testing for its adhesion to the wall.

It doesn't wiggle,
so Mrs. Monroe takes her drink and goes to bed,
unaware that her daughter isn't home.

"You can't die here unless the mirror wills it, Maia."

A great cloud of blackness swirls out from me, swallowing all in its path.

"So get June yourself."

ELEVEN

In the Dark

Lucy's voice breaks the heavy quiet. "Maia?"

"You've got a lot of explaining to do," Rylee says to the darkness.

Maia stands and gropes around at knee level for Lucy's shoulder. She helps the girl to her feet. "We don't have time for explanations, Rylee. We need to get out of here."

"Where's June?" Lucy grips Maia's arm. She looks around as if she'll be able to see anything. "She was with us before—"

There's a shuffling of fabric as Rylee stands. She reaches blindly until she bumps Lucy's shoulder. "June's worst fear is being forgotten—"

"I know," Maia says.

Rylee squints in the direction of Maia's voice, the expression lost to the heavy darkness. "How do you know that? You left before we had that conversation."

"What conversation?"

"At the sleepover. Right before we broke the mirror."

Maia sighs. "June's had the same fear for her entire life. When she was little, she would always ask her mom questions about her dad. You know—she never met him. Her mom would always say she didn't remember anything about him, and that's where the conversation would end. It terrified June."

"That's awful," Lucy whispers.

Rylee's eyes widen. "You don't think Noire will make us forget June, do you?"

"Or maybe June will forget *us*," Lucy says.

"No." Maia's decisive non-whisper is jarring in the darkness. "Noire doesn't have that kind of power."

My brows pinch together. She says it as if she *knows* I don't have that kind of power.

"Come on, we need to go."

"Go? *Go?*" Lucy's voice is shrill. "Go where, exactly? And how? And without June?"

Maia speaks through her teeth as she fumbles for her friends' arms. "I never said without June. It's all of us or none of us, right?"

It was something June had said to Lucy on the first day of ninth grade, just after Lucy admitted that she'd moved because her school bullies got so bad:

Well, that won't happen again, June promised. *It's all of us or none of us now—*

Yeah, and no one would dare *bully June,* Maia laughed.

She shuffles along slowly, directionless in the darkness, pulling Rylee and Lucy in her wake.

"There's nothing here," Lucy whispers. "Like, *nothing* nothing."

"Maia?" Rylee prompts. "How did it happen last time? The cave that led to Lucy's snake pit just kind of … built itself around us. Did you do something to trigger it? Like, I don't know … accidentally press a button or something?"

Maia laughs, the sound disjointed and untethered. "A hidden switch? Noire isn't an amateur, Rylee. She controls this world. She controls *everything—*"

Rylee squeezes Maia's arm in solidarity. "You keep saying that. But she can't really control *everything*, right? I mean, she's not doing anything to us right now. I'm not a doll anymore, Lucy's not a snake—"

"Maybe she's making us have this conversation." Lucy's interruption cuts through the eerie silence.

"*Lucy,*" Maia and Rylee say in unison.

Maia's voice is chiding.

Rylee's is breathless with fear.

"Shhh," Lucy hushes them. "Listen."

Voices. Harsher than the sweet call of the dolls. They boomerang from side to side, from one ear to the other.

"Wait—" Maia whispers.

The sounds bounce closer before rebounding again.

"—I hear her."

"Noire?" Rylee asks tightly.

"*June.*"

A neon flicker cuts through the darkness like a lighthouse beam through a tempest, there and gone. The girls stumble away from it, and Maia frowns when they all back into each other.

"Did you see that?" she whispers.

"Yes," they answer.

"Where?"

Rylee and Lucy's answers are eerily identical: "Right in front of me."

Before Maia can voice her theory, three flashes of color pop into being—one right in front of each girl.

Faces.

Black as night. Speckled in glaring, incandescent neon.

They pop from existence as quickly as they popped into it.

A scream shatters the silence, coming from every direction at once, rising in pitch until it becomes the ringing in their ears.

The sound wave splinters the darkness, spewing jagged shafts of blinding purple.

From the lightning spawns a sharp geometry—the outline of a giant labyrinth:

Threateningly tall.

Walls of obsidian, polished to a high shine.

Limitless.

A vertical opening spreads with a rumble of thunder, spilling brilliant blue across the girls as it dwarfs them.

"We find June in there," Maia says.

TWELVE

The Maze

"I really, really hate this place." Lucy's whisper is hardly more than a breath of air.

The girls are slow to enter, creeping past the opening like they expect something to jump out and grab them. Some deep instinct pulls them away even as their urgency pulls them forward.

The ephemeral blue of the maze tick tick ticks like fluorescent lights flickering, barely bright enough to make out the girls.

Their dim reflections accompany them in the glossy walls, turning the group of three into an uncountable, shifting number.

Lucy is the first to walk into a pane of black glass. She puts her hands on it, leaving fingerprints as she pokes around until she finds its edge and can move past.

"What would a maze have to do with June's fear?" Rylee wonders aloud. Her voice shakes, and I suspect her speculation is more to maintain calm than it is to receive an answer. "And how can Noire hide her in her fear if it isn't even … a *thing?*"

Lucy walks into another obstruction nose-first. She rubs out the ache. "Is no one going to tell me what's going on here?"

"June is hidden here somewhere," Rylee explains simply, "like you were with the snakes. We need to find her—"

"Yeah," Lucy snorts. "For sure. Easy. Except for the fact that we can't *see anything*—"

I take my cues well:

The space lights in a brilliant white, so sudden and bright that Lucy shrieks; Rylee presses the heels of her palms into her eyes; Maia blinks, eyes watering.

I pull up a seat and a glass of champagne for the coming show.

The blinding light fades into a series of pinpricks, mimicking the static, glitching colors of a TV without a program. Reflected in the walls, the floor. Stretching into the darkness far above.

Lucy screams and stumbles backward.

She takes out Rylee's ankle and smashes into Maia on the way down, and all three end up in a mangled heap on the reflective floor.

Lucy scrambles backward, knocks the back of her head into the wall behind her. Maia and Rylee look to see what spooked her and are greeted with just enough light to see their own reflections staring back from the black glass.

Maia exhales sharply. "Come on," she says, readying to stand. "Let's go get June."

"No, stop—" Lucy reaches past Rylee and grabs Maia's shoulder. I can see her fingernails dig in from here.

Rylee looks between the two of them. "What?"

"They're there."

"*Who's* there?"

"The … things. The ones that took us."

"It's just us, Luce. Our reflections." Maia gets to her feet.

Lucy follows. "It's not. Look closer."

Maia and Rylee study their reflections again:

Rylee smoothes her doll's frock as she stands.

Maia narrows her eyes.

Lucy's reflection is smiling, staring directly at them.

Lucy is not.

At once, like someone flipping the switch of a two-way mirror, their reflections are replaced by a thousand staring faces.

Creatures, in the purest sense of the word.

shaggy strange abominable
freakishsegmentedgarish
lithe angular sleek savage
wild willowy grotesque
exquisite

A myriad of bodies, each one
different
better
worse than the last.

"Run," Lucy breathes. "Run!"

Maia catches her with an arm around her shoulders, nearly clotheslining the poor child. She turns Lucy around and releases her. "They're not chasing us."

They're hardly even breathing.

They just stand there, staring.

"Why aren't they moving?" Rylee whispers, voice so quiet even I must strain to hear it.

June's shape flashes in the polished obsidian, there and gone; a patchwork of transparency.

Recognizable only by the scar on her knuckles from the metal frames of Tommy Williams's glasses and the friendship bracelet Lucy gave her in ninth grade.

The blood drains from Maia's face.

"June's forgetting *herself*," she says.

"I thought Noire couldn't do that—"

"She's not. The *mirror* is doing this."

A peal of warning sounds in my head.

"Excuse me?" Lucy frowns.

"This place—this ... this *thing* is like a virus. You step in even for a minute and the mirror reaches into your mind. It mirrors it. It takes all your fear and your negativity and reflects it until it breaks you—"

Maia rounds on Rylee, her eyes wild. "Neural connections—" she demands.

Rylee steps back, bewildered at Maia's suddenly sharp tone.

"We learned it last year, Ry—how many neural connections in the human brain? Average."

Rylee's answer is automatic: "100 trillion."

"Yeah. Yeah, yeah."

Maia moves through the maze at a clip that has her tapping on the walls to find their edges.

Rylee and Lucy try to keep up, throwing glances at each other.

"And now take all those connections and place them in here—in a world that fractures them and reflects them and the mind, it—it *expands*. Forever. People can't take that kind of pressure, Rylee."

The warning bell in my head rings clearer.

Maia's right.

The mirror doesn't just reflect what's in your own mind. It also reflects itself: projects the knowledge of the people it's absorbed, the thoughts it's consumed, the things it's seen until the mind cracks beneath the weight of knowing too much.

It's how—even unconscious—Maia knew about perfluorocarbon.

But she shouldn't know any of *that*.

She says it like it's indisputable.

Like she's known her whole life.

Maia picks up her pace.

She pulls ahead of Rylee and Lucy.

Their calls to *Wait!* quickly fade as her jog turns into a run.

Then a sprint.

I leave Rylee and Lucy to the maze because I can't shake the feeling that there's *something* about Maia.

She pushes herself harder harder harder—

Takes corners with such speed she has to slingshot herself around with a palm on one wall to avoid crashing into the next.

She calls June's name like the name itself might make the girl appear.

Maia screeches to a halt at the long hallway that stretches before her, dark but for the neon globes that light it irregularly.

A shape ripples at the far end.

Maia squints.

A shimmer—five-and-a-half feet tall, moves in the shadows. The neon glow of the hallway catches the speckles that litter its skin as it wavers.

"June?"

It turns, recognizing the sound of Maia's voice, displacing the neon around it.

Instinctively, Maia steps toward her friend.

The floor clicks beneath her foot.

Her face goes slack.

"You have *got* to be kidding me."

I laugh with unexpected glee at the reaction a simple button can evoke.

A shaft of light splits the blackness under Maia's foot: cracking, splitting, jumping. Branching toward the end of the hallway until it reaches June.

Her shape vacillates.

Maia lurches into a run. "Wait—"

The walls stretch until they creak and groan. The end of the corridor wavers, as though obscured by heat waves.

And then it *twists.*

Slowly, like wringing out a rag, the far end begins to rotate.

Maia's steps falter as the ground shifts beneath her feet, angling higher and higher until she loses her footing and rolls with the corridor's gradual twisting.

I pause it just long enough to allow her to get back to her feet, and she barks a sharp cry when it slips out from under her again.

She rolls with the movement, sliding on the smooth surface as she tries to get her feet beneath her.

She takes a step and topples to the right.

I laugh at my own genius and the way her frustration sounds as she struggles to reach her last friend.

June's form ripples.

And disappears.

Despair twists Maia's face.

She reaches the hallway's end and darts around the corner, feet faltering on the now-steady ground.

She slams her palms against a wall to catch herself mid-fall and puts on a burst of speed, lungs heaving like a blacksmith's bellows as her feet slap the floor.

"June!" she shouts, voice raw.

She runs past walls fragile as a house of cards—just translucent enough to see June on the other side, the corporeal form caught and pulled by the mirror's currents.

Too fast for Maia to keep up with.

"*June!*"

She slows to a stop, legs shaking. Great, gasping breaths heave through her raw throat as she bends over to put her hands on her knees. She screams behind her teeth, and I'm not sure if her frustration is with me or herself.

"*Fine*, Noire," she spits. "You want to play? Let's play."

She drops to a crouch and slams her palm against the ground.

The floor drops out beneath her.

Something in her peels away, and I catch the sense that she's hiding something from me.

From the mirror.

The maze, perfect as it was when she initially entered, regenerates around her.

June regenerates.

I stumble back a step.

She should not be able to do such a thing.

The control—the *practice* it takes to unwind and recreate even one of the mirror's creatures is severe.

Maia just regenerated an entire segment of the fabric of its *world*.

I throw up more walls around her, close her in.

She explodes through them with half a thought.

She sprints for June.

I splinter the ground between them.

Maia leaps, suspended in midair.

She slams into June, curls her body around her friend to protect her. Sharp, brittle pieces slice Maia's arms, her face, her right ear.

The maze shudders and cramps around them.

And together, they
crash
crash
crash
crash
crash
crash
crash
through its walls.

The mirror rips June from Maia's grasp like some great god closing a fist.

It discards the maze around her as she careens through open, empty air, pieces pixelated and glitching like an infected computer program.

My champagne glass slips from my fingers and shatters, spraying the ground with glittering gold as a chill of shock cracks down my spine.

The darkness that usually shrouds me slips away as I lose my grasp on it.

Something is *wrong.*

The mirror takes Rylee and Lucy too.

The only pieces that remain of my maze are particles of obsidian, glass, and silver—a vast Saharan wasteland that scatters the mirror's surface.

Maia instinctively covers her head as she slams into the detritus.

Her body tumbles over and over itself, kicking up sparkling shards, carving a path until she finally skids to a stop.

THIRTEEN

In Plain Sight

Maia lays on her side, back toward me, and finally gasps, the sound raw and aching.

She pushes herself up to kneeling—arms shaking, elbows like ungreased hydraulics—and flexes her hands that once held June.

Terror slices through her when she doesn't see Rylee or Lucy or the maze, either.

"No. *No!*"

There's that word again.

She searches on her hands and knees, fingers frantic as they sift through the glassy sand.

Her face crumples like metal under pressure.

She was winning. She was so *close.* She'd almost beaten my game.

But that's the thing:

it's not really my game.

And there is no winner but the mirror.

She stiffens when she spots me.

For a stretched moment, all we can do is stare at each other.

And then a trickle of anger goes down the back of my throat.

She is not rejecting the mirror because she *fears* it.

"What are you hiding, Maia?"

The helplessness in her eyes transforms into fury. She scrambles to her feet and stalks toward me like a lion.

"*You,*" she snarls. "What have you done to them?"

The voice that comes out of her is not one I've heard before.

"What have you *done?*"

She shoves me so hard by the shoulders I stumble back a step.

I finally get a hold of myself when she lunges for another strike. I catch her wrists. *Squeeze.* Her bones creak within my grip.

Anger rises in me like a tide, and it isn't mine. "Sorry, Maia. Fighting is against the rules."

"Rules?" Her voice is a live wire as she shoves away from me, ripping her wrists from my grasp.

"*Rules?*" Her eyes are wild, unhinged as she paces like a caged animal. "What *rules?!*"

"Mine."

She halts mid-pace and turns on me—a predator hearing the snap of twigs—the evidence of its prey.

A foreign chill creeps up my neck from the very base of my spine.

She shoots a hand forward, and from the empty space to my left, glass shatters, as if she's cracked a part of the mirror world itself.

I duck to the side.

A piece in the spray nicks my cheek.

I reach up and smear the warm trickle with my fingertips.

A laugh bubbles from the base of my throat at the smudge of blood, wild and feral and for the first time in an eternity: undisciplined.

Unnerved.

I hear the snap and pop of glass under pressure before the air in front of me ruptures.

My laugh grows wilder.

I dance back from Maia as she stalks toward me, steering my path with sprays of sharp fragments.

The hysterics come all the way from the bottom of my belly as I laugh and laugh and laugh and *laugh*—

Maia's eyes glow violet with her rage.

She times her words with each out-casting of her hands—left, right, left, right—

"You. Promised. You'd. *Let. Them. Go*—"

She freezes.

Every vein, every muscle halts in action, caught in the mirror's hold.

It may not be sentient,
but it can neutralize a threat.

And though it's not cognizant like a human, it is akin to a hound: loyal until threatened.

It has a soft spot for me.

And I suspect the only reason it doesn't crush Maia right now is because it has one for her, too:

On a very, very short leash.

My frenzy abates, and I step toward her.

A tremor goes through her outstretched arm. Her eyes are the only thing that move as she tracks me.

"I never promised anything."

The mirror releases her, and Maia crumples to her knees.

When she doesn't immediately get up, I take another step nearer. Her face is hidden by a curtain of matted hair, still damp from the lake.

Her shoulders tremble, then shake.

She sniffs.

Pity is a thing I've long forgotten, and its sudden appearance is as startling as my earlier madness.

An uncomfortable feeling of humanity sits on my shoulders.

"Oh, you poor, tiny thing." I kneel beside her.

She lets out a harsh sob and buries her face in my shoulder. Alarm roots me in place.

I sit perfectly still, afraid that if I move, I might scare her away.

A kinship glows orange at the base of my rib cage.

Perhaps I underestimated her. Perhaps, like me, she won't unravel beneath the mirror's pressure.

Perhaps I won't be alone here anymore.

"It hurts," she whimpers.

I blink back my surprise.

Not just at the sharp turn of emotion, but at the way the connection between us goes strikingly cold.

I shift beside her and raise a hand to pat her shoulder …

And hesitate.

There's a feeling that surrounds her like an electric fence; harmless, until it isn't.

I tap my fingertips against her, reluctant at first, and it's as if I imagined the danger, because it isn't there now.

I wrap my hand around her shoulder and squeeze her into my side in an embrace I'd long given up wishing for. "It hurts because you're rejecting it. You can admit it to me, you know—that you want to stay."

"What if I don't?"

"Oh, but you do."

She sniffs.

"You can tell me how this place has called to you since the day you abandoned it."

She tucks her knees into her chest. Wraps her arms around her legs and rests her head.

"I'm tired." Her voice is muffled. "I'm angry. I want …"

Her shoulders rise and fall.

"I *want*," she says, and there's that feeling again: an electric charge before the storm.

I squeeze her tighter into my side. "Everything will be okay." I shiver, suddenly nervous. "You can stay—like I have. If you don't fight it, it won't hurt you."

A giggle surprises me, so reminiscent of the child I once was.

"You can stay and play."

She lifts her head.

Smiles at me.

And all at once, she stops fighting.

I feel her let go like falling from a cliff backward, arms outstretched to feel the air rush by.

Her mind and memories open like a gaping maw and suck me into the vortex.

And I see her for what she truly is:

A liar.
An actress.
A *fraud.*

FOURTEEN

Bravo, Maia

She only ever showed me what she wanted me to see, and now she peels back every layer, flinging me though memories and thoughts and reasons and cues in much the same way the puppet strings tossed her:

She stands in the snow as a 7-year-old child, watching her parents' caskets lowered into the frozen ground.

Adults tell her everything will be alright. They handle her with caution, as though she's too young to understand such a heavy concept.

And though she smiles and nods, all she wants to do is scream. Even at seven, she begins to comprehend that the only thing she will ever hold control over is herself.

The hunger for it grows exponentially: shows itself in her painfully clean room and her cracked knuckles from washing her hands too much and the fits she throws when her grandmother misplaces her things.

The mirror sees her hunger for control the moment she enters its world for the first time. Rips it apart and feeds it back to her in fragments, the edges splintered and jagged.

She escapes and locks down every emotion she can find—her fear, her joy, her sorrow.

Anything that can make her lose the control she fought so hard for she packs tightly away in a neat little box.

She stands in a hospital room as a steady beep declines to a flatline, and life takes her grandmother from her as well.

She learns to project what she can no longer feel. Her sharp mind misses nothing, even at ten:

She watches people—learns the expressions they make, the emotions they feel, and mirrors them at just the right times:

She learns to hide things, to manipulate.

She plays me. For seven years.

She knows about our connection from the beginning and uses it against me.

She purposely fails classes—is average in every way to distract from her true cunning.

She fakes her panic attack in junior high just to remove the mirrors from her house. Tells the school therapist she has *eisoptrophobia*—a word she learned from the mirror itself.

She maintains a distance between herself and her friends, because they're the only things she allows herself to care about. The only things that can break her.

Maia reconstructs her memory of their last party around me. I stand once more in Mrs. Monroe's antique mirror.

The memory of Maia stands at the far edge of the attic, as far from me as she can get.

She feels my attention pull into my own thoughts; knows I am not watching her so closely.

So instead, *she* watches *me.*

She is the thing that pulls at the space between us, tightening it like a spoke.

Her friends swing pillows at each other with reckless abandon, heedless of the mirror in their midst.

She lodges herself between them and the mirror, convincing me of her fear to return.

She gets angry, leaves early.

But there is no anger.

And there is no fear.

There is only her projection of them. Her manipulation.

A *lie*, all of it.

She stomps down the street, yanks against the mirror's pull. She stands her ground outside just long enough to make me think it's the *mirror* that brings her back.

The reality is quite different: she somehow knows the taste of the mirror's pull so intricately, she shoves it back through the gateway that binds us, and I am none the wiser.

She feels my attention slip away to focus on Rylee, June, and Lucy—just arriving in the mirror world—and uses that time to take a breath. To wait.

It was never a slow, painful journey back to the mirror.

It was a calculated one.

She feels two distinct things in the empty attic:

Horror at herself—because there's a part of her that still believes she isn't capable of something like this—that comes from somewhere deep inside—a place she's locked down iron-tight.

And a twisted sense of overwhelming relief, because she didn't send her friends through herself.

The feeling is so alarming—so jarring in this moment that I almost miss the reason behind it:

She needs them for something.

She needs them *inside the mirror*, for something.

I am right here beside her, seeing the way she crafts her lies—every movement, every flicker of muscle in her face manipulated to show me only her fear in this moment.

She throws thoughts through our connection that drip with it like venom.

She enters the mirror world and locks herself down tighter than ever before, gritting her teeth against its reaching tendrils.

She's been aware of it from the beginning, holding it away from something.

It's why the connection between us has been so cold since her arrival.

Her dialogue and emotions so stiff.

She asks me things over tea like, "Is it sentient?" not because she *cares*, but because she needs to know if the mirror can *fight back*.

She catches hold of Rylee and anchors the girl, her voice a strengthening lifeline each time she says Rylee's name.

And then she reaches into Rylee's mind.

Closes a fist around my hold—the *mirror's* hold—and snaps it, using the slap to conceal what she really did.

My blood runs cold.

She knew about her power.

All she needed was a way to access it.

Everything she said, did, thought, *felt* was to push me—make me push back until she found something that might unlock it.

She nearly drowns in the snake pit.

Her human will to survive hands her the key.

And somehow

somehow

somehow

she already knows how to use her power.

But the mirror is there—cracking into her mind further and further, and she can't use her power without loosening the grip on herself.

So she keeps playing my game, testing the mirror through me, until the stakes are too high to ignore:

Until she feels the same cracking pressure in June's mind that she's felt in her own.

Her guard slips in her desperation to reach June, and the mirror increases its digging.

It feels Maia hiding something.

It rips June away.

Hides Rylee and Lucy and dissolves the maze as it peers into Maia with increased scrutiny.

And finally …

I look down at the echo of a girl, who even at nine was cunning enough to agree to play my game …

Because she needed me
to look the other way.

Maia finally releases me.

I stagger beneath the weight of her secrets, her deception, her lies.

The Maia I look at now is not a Maia I know.

I square my shoulders.

"Bravo, Maia."

"I learned from the best."

"Why all of this?"

In answer, she only repeats the same thing she said after rescuing Lucy:

"The game isn't over yet."

This time her voice is smooth. Even. Controlled.

A lie—all of it.

Everything she is and ever was.

I see it all.

Almost all.

There's a small dark box at the back of her mind, entirely solid.

No lid, no latch.

Its panes are reflective, the edges sharp. It lurks in the recesses, unassuming and coldly silent.

"What's in the box, Maia?"

"It's not important."

"I do not like being lied to. And neither does the mirror."

"That's too bad, isn't it?"

She takes a step toward me.

I take a step back.

"Where are my friends, Noire?"

The mirror reveals them to me in fragments: frozen in the moment before it ripped them away.

Find out what she's hiding, it presses.

I pull back the darkness that hides the girls from Maia.

Maia reaches for June.

I grab her wrist.

"I will ask only once more, Maia Hartley: What's in the box?"

"Wouldn't you like to know?"

I purse my lips.

Uncurl my fingers from her wrist.

"Say your goodbyes."

FIFTEEN

Not Going Home

The mirror releases June, restores Rylee and Lucy, resets their memories, reconstructs the maze, and I step back into the shadows to watch, so uncertain of what comes next.

Rylee and Lucy slam into Maia so hard she rocks back a step. Relief tangles their arms around her.

June stands apart, shaking off the mirror's hold.

None of them can see me—still here. Right at Maia's side, where I belong.

Maia smiles, an unnerving thing.

There's a growing hum in her mind that drowns out their voices, echoes the pounding of her heart, ramping up and up and up and up.

It says: *I am not going home.*

It says: *I am home.*

From the side, cutting through the celebration like a hot knife through butter, June's voice: "What do you mean you're not coming home, Maia?"

The corner of Maia's eye twitches, face paling as her effort to hold off the mirror cracks her careful composure. "I—What?"

"I *said*"—June steps closer—"what do you mean you're not coming home?"

"I … don't—"

"You said it, just now. You said: 'I'm not going home.' "

The words catch Rylee and Lucy's attention, and they look at Maia, faces still glowing.

Their smiles melt like ice cream on a summer evening as Maia's smile flickers away.

"I … can't," she says carefully. "It's been seven years since the last time I was here."

Lucy, steps forward, quicker on the uptake than anticipated. "Wait, you mean—"

"Yeah … I mean."

"I really hope you're not saying what I think you're saying." June's voice is hard.

Maia looks at each of her friends, solemn. "I can't leave."

June spreads her feet like a fighting stance. "You're *not* staying here, Mai."

"I don't have a choice."

"You're just going to give up? That easy?"

"I'm not giving up—"

"You *aren't?*"

"I *can't leave*, June!" Maia's voice is tight as the mirror increases its pressure.

But it's also pleading—asking June to hear all the things she can't say.

To let her go, for now.

"I don't buy that."

"June—"

"You haven't even *tried*," June snarls. Even without seven years of the mirror's influence, her hostility matches Maia's. She's always been the tough one: her mother's cancer hasn't allowed her to be anything otherwise.

In the span of seconds, Maia calculates infinite possibilities, all of which halt at the same problem:

It will be all or none of them.

"Okay, okay." She softens her voice—bleeds the tension from her own shoulders.

I watch her shift into something that was once so familiar to me: the girl I followed for seven years.

"You're right," she says. "I don't know … not for sure. Let's try, okay? All of us or none of us, right?"

Maia's gaze flicks to me through the mirror's shadows.

I shake my head in warning.

Maia says: "Let's try."

SIXTEEN

Let's Try

"What exactly do you think you're doing?" I ask Maia from the shadows as Rylee, June, and Lucy tap on the walls around them, unaware of our conversation.

"It's better this way, that they think I'll fight to come back with them."

"You would let them believe something so cruel?"

"They won't have to believe it for long."

My form ripples.

"What?" she challenges, eyes cold. "You think I don't know what the mirror does to the people it takes? To their friends? Their families? You think I don't know by now how it makes them forget?"

It doesn't just make them forget.

The mirror erases the people it keeps from reality like deleting source code:

They dissolve from their friend's and family's memories; their fingerprints erase from the surfaces of things they touch.

As if they never existed at all.

Maia reads the thought as it crosses through my mind, and the look she gives me says she knows.

"They deserve a life out there whether I'm in it or not."

"The mirror will call them back," I warn. I don't know what I'm saying anymore. What I'm warning against. "Its changes have already begun. The real world will never accept them; it will be like trying to force pieces into the wrong puzzle."

"I know—"

"Maia!" Rylee shrieks.

I recoil further into the shadows as the mirror's creatures stir, tugging themselves from the maze walls, bleeding from the darkness.

One locks its eyes on Maia, and like a stone dropped in water, the motion ripples outward, turning each head until their reflective black eyes are pinned on her.

The mirror has found Maia's box.

“*Run*,” she whispers to her friends.

June snaps her gaze to her. “Where?”

“*Anywhere*.”

Walls slice up through the floor in the narrow spaces between the girls, separating them, only translucent enough to reveal their outlines.

“Maia!” Rylee pounds on the glass, eyes wide.

I turn my own wide gaze to Maia, feeling the signature of her power in these new walls.

The mirror pulses inward, the sound wave pressurized and severe.

Lucy is the first to scream, hands pressed into her temples. She drops to her knees. Rylee and June follow soon after, jaws hinged open in agony as the mirror bores into their minds—searching for anything that may hint at the thing Maia keeps hidden.

She cracks through the mirror’s pressure as easily as shattering glass, releasing her friends.

“*Go*,” she says. The pain in her eyes becomes clearer as the mirror returns its screaming attention to that box in the back of her mind. “I’ll come find you.”

She takes off, leading the mirror’s creatures away from her friends.

June gives a single, determined nod before turning to find her own way through the maze.

Lucy presses her hands to the thin obsidian that separates her from Rylee. "I don't want to be alone again," she whispers.

"I know, Luce. I'll come find you. Maia and June and I—We're going to go *home*, Lucy."

Lucy nods, slowly at first. "Okay. Yeah, home. Okay."

She takes a deep breath.

It's interrupted at its high point as hands reach from the blackness behind Rylee and yank her away.

Lucy screams, stumbles backward into a run.

Maia stops as the mirror's desperation multiplies. She puts a hand against the maze and bends in half, retching.

Everywhere June turns is a dead end. The maze boxes her in, constricting like a crumpled soda can.

The mirror's non-ground quivers beneath Lucy's feet. She skids to a stop, but her momentum is not quite so agile, and she nearly topples over the crevasse that yawns open.

She screams and presses her back to the maze, inches her feet away from the floor that crumbles beneath her.

Rylee flies backward, crashing through glass as hands grapple with her arms and legs and wrists and ankles.

A force blows her abductors away. Their touch disappears.

And so does everything else.

She hangs in the air, suspended as though in amber, and watches light from an unknown source bounce off the sleek splinters that float around her. The air is viscous, cold. Unrelenting as she attempts to swim through it—to right her buoyant limbs, place her feet back on the floor.

To even halt the rotation of her body that slowly turns the crown of her head toward the ground.

"Help," she squeaks, chest depleted of air even as she drowns in it.

"Help!" A little louder.

She floats higher from the ground as though pulled by invisible strings, flailing to catch any sort of traction in the syrupy air.

"Help!" she screams.

And across the maze, Maia's box

s p l i n t e r s

She's so distracted holding the mirror at bay, I take the opportunity to steal inside, unable to help myself.

There's little in here but a child, curled into the corner:

A young girl who never felt the mirror's hunger or craved its darkness.

My chest seizes.

The child frowns at the crack in the box and uncurls her legs. She approaches cautiously, but when nothing happens, she puts her face to the crevice and peers out.

The terror in her eyes when she realizes where she is—where she never really escaped from—is ice cold.

Like a box within a box, I view her thoughts through Maia's mind—separate from Maia's and yet the same.

Her small chest rises and falls rapidly as horror sinks in like ink through water:

She escaped one prison only to be trapped in another. One of her own making.

I want to turn away from the sight; make it untrue.

But I step past the girl, pulled by some unfamiliar force, and pick up the glittering thing that lays abandoned on the floor where she once sat.

As if she were put here to guard it.

Oh.

Oh.

Maia may have shut away her emotion—the fear that overwhelmed her child self—locked it conveniently in the same box.

But the child isn't what this stronghold was built to obscure.

The glittering thing in my hand is a memory, so compressed and concealed it's hardly viewable:

Mirrors.

In Maia's house.

Beneath her pillow.

I see the reasoning behind her manipulation—why she faked her fear of mirrors:

She couldn't have us watching her.

I should have seen it.

I should have *seen* it.

I step deeper into the memory, lift the corner of Maia's pillow.

Two broken shards of mirror are hidden beneath it, faced together—bound with not even a micron of space to spare.

It made it impossible for me to notice the rift—to look out at her world through it.

To feel her *learn* from it.

I peel the mirrors apart.

And from them spills Maia's secret.

A thing she's buried so deeply it's *ruined* her.

She plans to destroy the mirror.

And she needs her friends to do it.

The memories I watched just moments ago unravel further, pooling at my feet in webs:

Her escape, forbidden by the mirror, ripped her apart. It broke her until she could see only one option:

Break it back.

She didn't escape with a single piece.

She escaped with *two*.

One piece lodged in her mind, her soul: it's the thing that binds us.

The thing that allowed her to spy on the mirror.

On *me*.

She broke the other piece in half; stuck the shards together to create a way to absorb the mirror's knowledge without either of our notice.

She's been learning from it for seven years—as much as she could without being here.

Probing for weak spots.

Her earlier attack on me was nothing but a test.

A way to examine what the mirror would and wouldn't allow. She thought she might be able to weaken it by hurting me.

And she only softened when she realized it wouldn't let her.

She played me with her tears.

And she only revealed her true self when she confirmed I wasn't a threat.

"You *stupid* girl," I snarl. "It will kill us both for this."

"Then I guess you'd better help me."

The thought pulls a deranged laugh from my throat. "*Help* you?"

If *I* can see this, the mirror isn't far behind.

Even now, I can feel it probing deeper, its anger like nails on a chalkboard.

"Why would I help you, Maia? This place is my *home*."

"Because you want a friend."

My heart ceases its erratic beating.

"That's your whole thing, right? The reason you're so angry with me for not finding you seven years ago, right? You only wanted someone to *find* you—"

Maia's face locks down at something she sees in my expression.

She steps back from me. Folds her arms across her chest. "Let's be clear about one thing, Noire: you and I are not friends."

"Not yet," I whisper, my lips barely moving. It takes a few more tries before I can speak again. "What do you need them for? Rylee, Lucy, June?"

She allows me one last secret,
and I allow myself to peek.
Because she was right about me.

And I was so terribly, terribly wrong about her.

The secret peels open like flower petals, unfolding one by one until I see the truth. The last secret Maia hides:

There are cracks in the lining of this world.

Hairline fissures invisible to the mirror because of its greed.

Invisible to *me* because of my need.

The cracks splinter each time the mirror takes a human. Each time it lets one go.

Maia's forbidden escape cracked two solid pieces of it, and by bringing her friends in—three people all at once—

By helping them escape …

She's orchestrated everything from the beginning.
Everything.

She releases me from her hold, and the first thing I see is the violet ring in her eyes—almost swallowing them entirely now.

"Either help me, Noire, or get out of my way—"

She chokes.

The frightened child in the box is still a brave little thing—a fighter. She pounds her small fist against the walls.

Her scream is the sharp edge of glass.

With every strike, the fissure expands, expelling every emotion Maia locked away all these years.

The mirror squeezes its hold on Maia's friends, freezing them where they are, sound and movement and air ripped away as it targets them to get to her.

Lucy keeps her back to the wall, the deterioration of the chasm creeping closer to her toes.

Rylee's mouth is still open in her scream for help, fingers splayed toward the ground like she can ward it off if she falls.

June is mid-turn sideways, the maze so tight around her that her shoulders no longer fit.

A ticking sounds from beneath them.

Above them.

Around them.

It starts quiet
like the hands of a wristwatch
and grows in momentum
and volume
until it vibrates the air so wildly it shakes the girls loose from their gridlock.

Lucy's right foot begins to slip over the edge.

Rylee drops. Her scream follows her, unable to catch up to her momentum.

I halt her two inches from the ground.

She claws at it—pulls her body out of the viscous air to lay along the smooth reflective surface.

She so clearly wants to stay—to rest.

She's back on her feet in the same amount of time it takes Lucy to tiptoe past the crevasse on the thin strip of ground I unfold for her, and June to slip through the first opening of her slowly expanding prison.

I unravel the maze for them. Lead them to Maia.

And I ignore the way the mirror's anger turns toward me.

SEVENTEEN

Right Behind You

Maia grits her teeth and uses the rest of her strength to crack open a passageway.

The mirror convulses, its desperation making the rift unstable.

Through it, two separate worlds flash:

On one side: Reality.
The attic—slowly greying
with the early light of morning.

On the other: Fractals.
The light and lines of the mirror world
turning in upon themselves.

Maia shoves Lucy through first, face pinched in a grimace as she holds the line just long enough to get her friends out.

Lucy's knees buckle with the force of
her exit. She rolls across the attic floor.
Pulls herself to her feet to wait
for the rest of them.

"Maia," June says, sensing something amiss. In a rare moment of vulnerability, she asks, "You're coming with me, right?"

A wave of memory washes through Maia, forceful as a tsunami:

Washing the dried blood from June's knuckles in the school bathroom after the principal expelled her for breaking Tommy Williams's nose. Little white folded squares of paper they'd pass in the school hallways. Lying on Maia's bedroom floor, staring at the ceiling when June needed a break from the heaviness of cancer in her home.

Maia lets the wave soak her.

She smiles. A shadow of sorrow flickers in her gaze. "I'll be right behind you."

June pauses, as though something whispers of Maia's deceit. Then she nods. And she steps through the rift.

Maia pushes Rylee after her.

"Take care of them, Ry."

She says it so quietly I don't know if Rylee hears it before she shatters through the mirror.

Rylee's feet catch on the attic
rug and she pitches forward.
Lucy and June catch her
in a fierce embrace.

Maia stands exposed.

Alone.

As I am.

The child she locked away screams to be let out.

A crack fissures through her mind from the recesses, and I feel her reach inward to that little black box.

Ruptures stretch out from the main crevasse, expanding, spreading like a virus.

The child peers out with wide, terrified eyes.

She pounds on the sleek black surface with her palms, her fists, her knuckles. Every strike becomes more unhinged.

Each impact splinters the box further.

The mirror increases its pressure, crushing from the outside until it creates its own cracks.

Maia buckles to the ground and folds over her knees as she screams—presses the heels of her palms into her temples like she's trying to crush her own skull—to hold that box together if she has to do it with her own bare hands—thinking she just needs a little longer a little longer a little longer—

Fear bleeds from the box into Maia's veins like ice water as the child breaks free.

It stretches its little fingers into Maia's own.

And like a breach in the hull of a submarine miles beneath the surface, the mirror floods inside Maia's box.

EIGHTEEN

The End

It finds her secrets. Her plans. Her lies.

Its reaction is a screeching glitch, a screaming misfire.

I cover my ears and drop to my knees only to be trampled by the onslaught of creatures.

Solid, black, humanoid.

Their purest forms.

The mirror's taste for showmanship is lost beneath the weight of betrayal, and its creatures bleed from every shadow, converging on Maia like starving beasts.

The mirror may not be sentient.

But it can neutralize a threat.

Maia's box is in ruins, fear bleeding into every cell of her body.

The child she once was looks out through her eyes and spots the rapidly closing portal home, and my own blood runs cold as I realize what it plans to do.

It ducks the first creature and lunges.

The mirror yanks her back, stretching the distance between her and the gateway. The empty space between crowds with creatures.

A fist cracks Maia in the jaw, snaps her head to the side. She retaliates.

Every strike she throws is more technically precise, her muscles absorbing the memory of every fight the mirror has ever witnessed.

Every fighter it's ever consumed.

But the harder she fights, the harder the mirror fights back.

It matches her pace.

Its creatures match her blow for blow.

It reflects her desperation—drives it through her chest like a sledgehammer.

The childlike terror that fills her dissolves her precision—her cunning—her *plan*—and the way she fights crumbles from perfection into something pit-like, feral, visceral as she rips into the mirror's creatures with tooth and nail, frantic to reach the flickering rift.

June untangles herself from Rylee and Lucy.
She grabs Rylee's shoulders.
"Where's Maia?"
Rylee frowns like she doesn't understand.
"*Maia*, Rylee, where is she?
She was right behind you—"

June snaps her gaze to the mirror frame,
the rift inside an angry, swirling mass.

Maia drops into a low sweep, kicking the legs out from under several of the creatures.

She doesn't see the one on her right that lunges at her from a crouch.

Its shoulder crunches into her sternum as it knocks her off balance, sends her skittering.

I wish I could say I help.

Or hinder.

Or do anything at all.

The truth is that I can't move my body.

Shock holds me in place like a stake driven into the floor through my skull.

A creature grabs Maia from behind, ebony arms wrapped tight around her stomach. It flips her backward over its body, and I cringe at the sound her head and shoulders make as they hit the ground.

The creatures overwhelm her.

I see glimpses of her through their blackness.

And then I don't.

I can hardly breathe.

A seismic wave ripples from the center of the swarm, energy whining like a jet engine as Maia steps out from under them.

The ground splinters beneath her feet as she sprints toward the rift, crevices spreading behind her like veins.

She shoves her hand through, fingers brushing the boundary between worlds enough that June catches sight of her.

A creature drags her back and she shatters the thing with half a thought, screaming her failure and her fury at the child driving her, the emotion she worked so hard to bury, the control slipping slipping slipping through her fingers.

The pain of fighting not only the mirror, but a buried and forgotten piece of herself.

A thing that screams, *This is not who we are!*

It reaches through the boundary again—fighting, pushing, *clawing* at the mirror's hold.

It gets so close to breaking through that the child allows itself to *hope.*

And that's the kicker: that tiny fleck of wish.

It's the thing Maia grabs by the throat and *twists.*

She fractures herself into the mirror.

Becomes it.

That glowing, violet ring overtakes the once-soft brown of her eyes.

The lights in the attic flicker
revealing only pieces
of Maia's movements
turning her outstretched hand into a ghostly, glitching
r e a c h

June lunges for her,
fingertips brushing.

The lights go out.

When they flicker back to life,
Maia is gone.

The mirror's frame
is just a frame.

June stares at her empty hand
like she can't figure out what's
missing.

I watch it all from the pieces
scattered across the floor.

And for the first time in all the lifetimes I've lived,

I cry.

EPILOGUE

… or is it?

I stand on the shore of a cobalt ocean.

Maia pieces together beside me, power buzzing around her so strongly it lifts the hair on my arms.

The mirror is subdued, for now.

I'm a little awed.

A little apprehensive.

A little terrified.

I am—in feeling—six years old again.

I'm sitting at the foot of my mother as she sews, a fire crackling in the hearth.

I'm wishing for her to look at me with something other than anger.

I'm scurrying into my straw bed, more afraid of her lecture than I am of the creatures that crawl through the mirror I broke.

It was a gift from the queen to my mother.

I hated it.

And when I discovered the world within—the mirror that held onto me so tightly I couldn't leave if I tried—I never looked back.

I peek out at the world beyond, fracturing myself from this rippling ocean to every corner of the world.

People pass by in the billions, every ethnicity, every age.

Some stride by without a second's thought; some pause to check their reflections in the store windows I watch from.

It's raining someplace, droplets pattering into puddles, rippling my view.

No one sees me.

Their naïveté reminds me of my own, as a child:

I'd sprint through puddles, muddying the hems of my skirts, and not lend a single care to what may be watching from beneath their surface.

I would polish the silver daily, laugh with my young friends at our upside-down reflections in the spoons.

I'd pass the queen's bracelets and brooches and necklaces when my mother would drag me into the royal closet to dust, not even considering the hundreds of facets—the millions of angles—I could be watched from.

Of course, all those years ago, mirrors might not have been around long enough for anyone to watch *from.*

Maia's edges are lit in violet.

I clear my throat. "What now?"

Her gaze flickers to mine before she looks back at the horizon.

"That's the question, isn't it?"

Kenzie Dawn is a debut New Adult author from Salt Lake City, Utah. She spent her young years dreaming up stories on the bus to and from school, and her teen ones ignoring her teachers in favor of writing. When she's not writing, you can often find her reading, thrifting, or redecorating the house.

She currently lives in Houston, TX with her husband Kristopher and their cats, Mortimer Jones and Charlotte.

THE STORY CONTINUES

in 2023

Pre-order here!

STAY IN-THE-KNOW ABOUT UPCOMING WORKS:

kenziedawn.com

Enjoy MIЯROR?

I would love to hear your thoughts!

Email me at
kenziedawnauthor@gmail.com

Leave a review on Amazon, Goodreads, social media, or kenziedawn.com

PLAYLIST

ACKNOWLEDGEMENTS

I do believe I've worked harder on these than on the entire book. The book was given permission to be imperfect, but the acknowledgements must reflect the perfection of the support I've received.

You see the problem?

Special Thanks …

To Brooklyn Draudt, Ellie Hansen, Lily Huggard, Meggie Huggard, Kate Kirkham, Ali McClellan, Ellie Norman, Kaylee Poffenberger, Kora Stokes, Harmony Stuart, Melody-Ann Swanson, and Rachel Thacker for your insights into the characters that truly gave them life.

To Halli Burnett, Ruby Jones, Zoe Molino, Madison Phelps, Abbie Stokes, Isabella Stuart, and Brynlee Thompson for inspiring pieces of the mirror's creatures.

To Tammy Coleman, Emilie Fausett, Nate Hadley, Kayeli Hathaway, Shelby Hovley, Kyle Lawrence, Matthew Stokes, Landry Thomas, and Jeanne Voehl for inspiring aspects of the mirror world.

To Jaxon Hinds, Logan Stuart, and Rylee Bigler: You were some of the first people to reach out and say how excited you were to read the book—sometimes authors just need to be told. (And yes, Rylee, your name is in this book for a reason, and I'm so excited to hear that you're beginning to write as well!)

To my beta readers: JoAnna Hubbard, Brenda Nickell, and Kathleen Rogers for your insights and advice.

With extra-special thanks to Spring Taggart Scoville, who wasn't afraid to ask the hard questions, and without whom this book might have been published as a shitty first-draft, and Kylee Haueter, who talked me through my imposter syndrome every time I saw her for a solid month.

To Shelby Hovley, Ken Hovley, and *The Altitude* for the incredible images, reels, and videos connected with this story.

To C.R. Jane, for taking the time to walk me through self-publishing on Amazon, even when crazy busy with her day job and her own seemingly impossible deadlines.

To Jeff and LeeAnn Zappitello, who stepped in to speed-read this novel and offer suggestions when writer's block struck.

To my mother, Ann Andreasen, for her continued support and unending love.

To my father, Matthew Andreasen, who provided word substitutions when I was 110% burnt out and multiple long, late-night phone calls (and a few all-nighters) to perfect this story.

To my husband, Kristopher, who made sure I would always say the word *mirror* correctly (mir-ror).

To the little girl who would sit on the school bus and dream up stories to music:

We did it. We made it.

And finally, to my readers:
This story wouldn't exist without you.

Made in the USA
Middletown, DE
12 March 2023